Tony C

LOST IN TIME

DOUBLE DRAGON

ACKNOWLEDGEMENT

For my friends Glen and Carla Ashton

ACKNOWLEDGEMENT

For my friends Glen and Carla Ashton

Chapter One

Gordon awakened as an electric shock of danger surged through his body.

He lay completely frozen in the strange surroundings of the hotel room, straining to listen.

Total darkness engulfed him. He glanced quickly around the room, but all was still and silent. And yet, something had awakened him. His heart hammered against his chest so hard it seemed certain the sound could be heard all the way into the hall.

And though every fiber in his body screamed for him to jump up and flee, he forced himself to stay completely still.

Seconds passed like an eternity ...

From out of the darkness, the walls groaned and creaked horribly from every direction.

In the next second, total silence enveloped everything again.

A tidal wave of emotions swept though him as the eerie silence closed in around him like an invisible vise. In seconds, waves of fear and excitement and every emotion in between subsided into a single, all-consuming feeling.

He knew what was coming next.

That absolute certainty filled him now -- déjà vu, the feeling that he'd been here before -- and he knew what would happen next.

Again, the eerie creaks and horrible groans rose quickly to a heart-pounding crescendo. All around his bed, the darkness was filled with unseen activity.

And it all suddenly stopped.

They were in the room with him now.

He braced himself.

Gordon Smith threw off the covers and leapt toward the door.

From every direction, the 'Shadows' moved and reached for him.

"Away! Get back!" he shouted as he fumbled with the locks.

He felt their cold grip on his ankles and heard the whirring of their wings directly behind him.

Gordon turned and flailed at the darkness filled with Shadows as he kicked at the others below. Their pincer-like grasp fell away as he stared at the darkness.

At the edge of his vision, the darkness writhed with Shadows.

In a single movement he turned and threw back the last bolt and ran outside, pulling the door closed behind him.

He ran toward the stairs with a quick glance back.

The Shadows poured out from around the edges of the door and flew after him!

"Help! Anyone! Help!"

But he knew the futility of his cries even as he uttered them. He knew that all the people asleep in each room had a Shadow sitting over their faces, sucking at their breath and keeping them each in a state of deep unconsciousness while their Shadow brethren attacked him.

He ran!

As he took the stairs three at a time, he felt them

flying around him in the darkness.

Tiny, viselike fingers reached for his arms and legs. He let go of the railings to push them away.

And instantly stumbled, then missed the next step, and fell forward to the landing on the second floor in a heap.

The Shadows covered him in a writhing blanket of half-seen movement. He felt their tiny hands all over his body as they sought to hold him down.

He couldn't let them pin him. If they did, he knew something more sinister waited in the darkness to come and finish the job.

Gordon flung himself up with his arms flailing and legs kicking.

The Shadows screamed their fury as they bounced off the walls.

He ran down the last flight of steps in two bounds.

He sprinted through the darkened foyer toward the street outside. Without warning he crashed straight into a small end table, fell onto it and crushed it into pieces. Gordon leapt forward, rolled head over heels and bounced right up. He was smiling to himself at his acrobatic recovery when he suddenly smashed his toes into a chair leg.

"Ow!" He fell to the floor, holding his injured toes.

The Shadows suddenly flew down the last steps and came at him.

Gordon rushed forward and flung the door open.

The street was empty at three in the morning. And worse, a hazy fog filled the night air with an eerily floating cloak of evil.

Worse and worse!

Or was it?

He looked down at himself and felt a tiny sense of relief.

Well, at least he had on more than just his underwear -- he hated it when he was chased by the Shadows wearing only his underwear.

Of course, pajamas were only tolerably better.

And the only other item on his body was the leather necklace holding the key to his 'Time Transporter.'

"Just great!" he muttered out loud.

Everything was ruined now.

He actually had a ticket, a press pass actually, for the royal wedding of the Prince of Wales and Lady Diana tomorrow -- the storybook wedding of all times. And, he had so wanted to see it in person for once!

The Shadows shrieked behind him.

And worse, Sarah wasn't here to help him.

She was probably on a quiet, country walk with Jane Austen at this very moment ... this moment relatively speaking, hodge-podged somewhere within the infinite threads of the vast circuitous rivers and oceans that comprise the eternity that is the space-time continuum.

Or, something like that.

His memory was a bit fuzzy at the moment -- this moment in time ... here in *this time* ...

He *felt* the Shadows closing.

Gordon raced into the foggy London night with the Shadows right behind him.

The chase was on again, as it had been for as

long as he could remember.

And remembering, well, that was a bit nebulous as well -- almost as nebulous as time traveling. His memories were as jumbled as the times he'd visited -- they had no beginning and they had no end.

The only thing he knew for certain was the chase. He had to run; he must never get caught.

But it seemed no matter where they ran, the Shadows always found them and the chase began anew.

And one fact became dreadfully clear: the Shadows were getting closer to catching them each time.

But as much as the chase brought anxiety and fear, another fact brought him comfort to counteract it: Sarah Nightingale.

He wasn't in this alone -- well, he was this time. But, most of the times ... he wasn't.

That one, sure, comforting thought filled his heart with courage.

The next, logical progression of thought was just as certain though not comforting in the least.

Gordon Smith and Sarah Nightingale were being chased throughout time ...

But now, they had a plan.

He ran into the night as the wet, wispy folds of the fog engulfed him.

The Shadows shrieked with joyous terror.

Frantically, his mind raced as he ran faster. He had to find a place to make a stand and fight the Shadows off. And then, he would have to get to the Time Transporter and leave this time -- before the greater danger appeared.

The shrieks roared all around him as shadowy wings fluttered against his arms and back while he ran.

The fog and the night swallowed him whole as he raced down the London street. And yet, he couldn't get away no matter how hard he tried.

Gordon suddenly turned and raced down a side street. The darkness closed in as even the hazy streetlights disappeared.

He felt something on his back. But even as he twisted to throw it off, he felt tiny arms wrapping themselves around both his legs.

Gordon screamed and kicked frantically while still running.

He stumbled and lost his balance.

He twirled around, slashing out with his arms, trying in vain to dislodge the hated things off his back.

Gordon didn't realize it, but he'd stumbled out the side-street and back out on another main street.

"Off me! Get off me!"

In the next instant, Shadows lunged from every direction. He felt them all over him now. He threw some off only to have two more attach themselves like shadowy leeches.

They were all over him.

He screamed as they forced him down onto the cold asphalt.

The Shadows writhed all over him as they beat their wings to hold him place.

They pressed his face against the hard street. He felt their clammy skin all over his body now as they shrieked with delight at their victory.

He tried to struggle, but each time more Shadows pressed against him.

He couldn't move.

Suddenly, the sound of footsteps echoed in the darkness.

Gordon cringed against the inevitable.

The footsteps grew closer until he felt them right beside him.

"We have you at last, Gordon!"

He felt his heart sink.

Of course, he'd been caught before. But, this was the first time he'd been caught alone. Sarah had always been there to help him. And of course, he had rescued Sarah when she'd been caught.

"Your precious Sarah cannot help you this time!"

Gordon looked up.

The cloaked form standing above him laughed. And as he watched the creature laughing at him, it pulled back the hood that covered its head.

The faceless head stared down at him, laughing harder.

Gordon stared at the silver skin crisscrossed with diagonal lines across the featureless face.

"Who are you?" Gordon struggled against the Shadows' relentless grip.

"I am Anon."

"Just you? Or all of you?" Gordon had seen others of his kind chasing him in other times.

"We are the mighty Anon."

"Sounds a bit like a rock band."

The Anon raised his arm high above his head.

Gordon saw the glowing staff in its grip. And at

the end of the staff, around a glowing golden globe, miniature bolts of electricity sizzled and danced and made the air hum and crackle with power. And every few seconds, at irregular intervals, sparks erupted into the air.

Gordon recognized the staff -- all the Anon carried them. And all of them used them as some sort of weapon, though neither he nor Sarah knew for sure how.

He nodded at the staff as a shower of sparks blossomed again.

"You ought to get that fixed."

The Anon laughed crazily.

"Really, that can't be good -- giving off sparks like that."

"I am going to use it and send you into the vortex."

"Hmmm, doesn't sound all that bad."

"I will send you into time -- lost in time!"

"Well, that certainly doesn't frighten me. You see, I'm kind of lost in time already." Gordon chuckled.

The Shadows shrieked and held him tighter.

"No! You don't understand!" The Anon leaned over him until his silvery, featureless face almost touched his own.

Gordon felt a sudden panic.

"You'll be totally alone. Sarah will have no way to find you. And, you'll have no way to leave -- your Time Transporter will still be here! You will be lost and trapped until the day you die!"

Gordon groaned.

Sarah -- her laughter, her wit, her

14

companionship, her love -- made life worth living. She made everything fun, interesting and exciting. And most important, she was the one constant in his life as they bounced from time to time.

She was always there.

Without her, life would be ... unbearable.

And, without his Transporter ... he would be lost forever ...

Gordon struggled mightily against the tiny Shadows, but they pressed him down like thousands of tiny vises.

He couldn't escape.

"And now, we shall bid you adieu. The chase has been grand. But alas, now it has come to an end ... for you!" The Anon raised his silver face to the night sky and laughed out loud.

Gordon looked frantically around, searching for something, anything, that might help him escape.

But the fog cloaked street was empty.

The Anon straightened as he stopped laughing. The eyeless face stared down at him.

Gordon tensed, watching the staff coming toward him.

The Shadows howled into the night air as the electric bolts crackled and leapt higher around the glowing globe on the end of the staff.

"No!" Gordon shouted.

The Anon turned his head.

Suddenly, blinding spotlights cut through the night fog and filled the air with light. In the next second, screeching tires and the blare of a horn deafened them all.

Gordon closed his eyes as he realized the car

wouldn't have time to stop before it ran over them all.

The screeching of tires and the acrid smell of burnt rubber filled his senses.

And then, all was silence.

Gordon lay there a moment, afraid to move. But, when he realized he was still alive -- and that the Shadows no longer held him down -- he opened his eyes.

The car's front bumper was right above his face.

He rolled to his right and sat up.

"All right, what's going on here, eh?"

Two police officers stepped out of the car.

Gordon looked around quickly.

Of course, the Shadows had fled. They couldn't bear bright light. But, the Anon ...

Gordon spotted him lying on the road. The car had struck him and sent him flying.

As he watched, the creature rose up, pulling his black cloak tight around his shoulders.

"C'mon then, be careful. You've just had a nasty blow there," the policemen on his right said. "Just lie there until we get an ambulance."

The Anon rose to his full height, obviously unhurt. He raised the crackling staff towards the first policemen.

"Careful there, Johnny! He's got some kind of weapon!" the other policemen cried out as he pulled out his baton.

In the next moment, the Anon aimed the staff and lightning bolts leapt across the night air and engulfed the policeman, who screamed as the bolts of electricity grew thicker until the very air around

16

him glowed.

And suddenly, he was gone.

The other policemen retreated with a gasp. He grabbed a spotlight mounted on the car window and switched it on. The beam hit the Anon square.

"The lights!" the Anon shouted as he turned and ran.

Gordon jumped up and ran in the other direction.

Behind him, he heard the policemen calling for backup on his radio.

At the next corner, he checked the signs. He smiled. He was almost there.

And none too soon, either.

The fog and darkness surrounded him again, and he heard the wings of the Shadows as they sought him out. And the Anon would not be far behind.

He just needed a few more minutes!

He reached the next alley and turned down it.

It was just a common dead-end little alley, like thousands throughout the city. The alley was empty, devoid of anything. And at the far end, the brick wall signaled he could go no further.

Gordon slipped the key off around his neck and held it up to eye level.

The outline of a door shimmered in the air, and when it grew solid it opened right before him.

Gordon jumped inside and shut it.

The door disappeared again.

He searched hurriedly inside his Transporter. He threw objects off the shelves and jumped to another row and searched again. He had to hurry; they mustn't know he'd been inside.

17

"Aha!"

He rushed back, inserted the key -- and it opened. Outside, the foggy night beckoned.

Gordon raced out and waved the key at the air behind him. The door closed, and again the Transporter was invisible.

He heard the sound of wings in the air.

"Oh no! I'm stuck!" he shouted with emphasis.

The air filled with moving Shadows seconds later.

He waited for them.

They swept over him and again pinned him down. As he feigned to struggle, he made sure his hand concealed the small object.

He turned toward the sound of running footsteps.

"Hold him!" the Anon shouted. "We must be quick and leave this place!"

"Ah now, don't be in a rush and all," Gordon chided.

"Silence!"

Gordon smiled.

The Anon twisted his head in puzzlement. He raised the crackling staff and slowly turned it toward Gordon, the bolts of energy leaping ever higher.

Gordon flicked the switch on the omni-torch he held and opened his hand.

The light was a hundred times brighter than the policeman's spotlight. And although it fit comfortably within the palm of his hand, it flooded the entire alley in a bath of white light.

The Shadows cried in agony and pain as they

fled.

The staff fell from the grasp of the Anon as he stumbled backwards in shock.

"Now then, let's have a look at this."

Gordon picked up the staff.

"No!"

The Anon rushed at him while he covered his face with one hand.

Gordon pointed the staff, and bolts of miniature lightning leapt out. They surrounded the Anon until the air glowed around the creature.

And suddenly, he was gone.

"Well now, it works on them too." Gordon laughed.

Farther down the street, sirens wailed.

"Oh well, I guess I'll have to miss the wedding anyway." Gordon stood up with the staff in his hand. He flicked the switch on his omni-torch, and the alley returned to darkness.

"I'll just have to amuse myself at the dance." He smiled a moment. "In fact, I'll ask Miss Austen if she'll give me the pleasure of having the first dance with her."

Chapter Two

Gordon stepped out of thin air and onto the open field of swaying grass.

He turned and twisted the key, and the door disappeared again. He smiled as he took a deep breath of the fresh country air.

"Ah, there's nothing as beautiful as the English countryside."

Gordon wore a top hat, a dark blue coat with a matching silk waistcoat, buff trousers and high boots. As he walked confidently toward the lane with his walking stick in hand, he looked a striking figure -- the perfect appearance for a gentleman of the eighteenth century.

And indeed, that was the time.

The birds sang gaily as he walked alone along the country lane. In fact, the only sounds were the rustle of the leaves in the light breeze and the happy singers flittering from tree to tree around him. He breathed deeply the fresh air and smiled each time a bird sang out.

After he had walked a couple of miles, a great manor house came into view on the rise of the hill before him. He quickened his pace, and soon the details of the house and grounds came into perspective.

The house was rectangular overall and built with sturdy brick. It stood three stories with stone chimneys rising above the slate roof like slender towers. Approaching the front of the grand house, he now noticed the substantial gardens. Gordon quickly realized the season must be late summer --

the garden literally seethed with riotous waves of colors that indicated flowers at their peak of beauty.

His heart beat faster when he saw the numerous carriages parked in the front. Yes, the dance was tonight. But most important, his Sarah would be there.

And she would no doubt be accompanied by her new friend, Jane Austen.

The manor house was even more impressive up close -- it rose like a small castle before him. In front, a few small groups of men and women walked along the brick paths that wound leisurely through the vast garden. The evening air was laden with fragrance as other brightly dressed ladies and gentlemen made their way to the front door.

Gordon Smith quickly made his way to the main entrance of the manor.

"Ah, there he is."

Gordon recognized Sarah's sweet voice instantly amid the happy chatter around him.

She walked toward him arm-in-arm with Miss Austen.

Sarah's sandy blonde hair was put up in a fashionable style of the period. Gordon noticed how her blue eyes sparkled as she drew neared. She wore an empire waist green dress that complemented her figure, and he noticed a small gold necklace around her neck.

Sarah's beauty took his breath away at times. Her face was shaped delicately, like fine china. And as beautiful as her face, her eyes were most distinctive.

Gordon loved her eyes -- she had sad eyes -- the

way they were shaped seemed to give her a permanent hint of sadness if you looked only at her eyes. And yet, her usually cheerful countenance and witty humor made her sad eyes quite a paradox.

In fact, many things seemed a paradox when it came to his beautiful Sarah.

"So, this is your young man," Jane said with an appraising glance.

"Miss Austen, may I present my good friend, Mister Gordon Smith."

Gordon took Jane's hand and bowed to kiss it gently.

He released her gloved hand and turned to take Sarah's hand.

Their eyes made contact. And in that instant, he felt a jolt of emotion.

Her smile disappeared.

"Are you all right?" Sarah asked with concern. She looked him over a moment. "You've had some trouble, haven't you?"

"A little, yes. But, I'm here in one piece." He could never hide anything from her.

Jane looked from one to the other. "My, you do know each other intimately. I mean, for Sarah to discern so much simply from a glance -- and after you've been parted for a time too."

Gordon and Sarah laughed.

He now took Sarah's hand and kissed it firmly.

He felt Sarah catch her breath at their shared touch.

"Could you excuse us a moment, dear Jane? I must speak in private with Mr. Smith." Sarah reached out and squeezed Jane's hand.

"Of course, my dear, but please don't delay too long. The first dance is due to start on the hour."

Gordon pulled a pocket watch out of his waist coat pocket and checked the time. "Well, that gives us ten minutes then."

"We'll see you inside." Jane turned away.

Sarah and Gordon walked side by side away from the crowd.

"I must say, I'm as impressed as Jane." Gordon smiled at Sarah. "How could you tell from just a glance I'd been in a bit of trouble?"

"Well, it could be woman's intuition. Or, as Jane hinted, that we know each other so well I can tell at a glance when something is wrong."

"I like the latter reason best." Gordon chuckled.

"Or ... it could be that hint of a bruise on your forehead and those tiny scratches on the back of both your hands where you've had to fight off Shadows that tipped me off." Sarah stopped and crossed her arms defiantly.

Gordon paused and shrugged in reply.

"I told you before, Gordon, I don't like us time traveling apart like that. And see, I was right. Those nasty Shadows jumped you and slashed you with their filthy talons enough to hurt you."

Gordon sighed. "Actually, they caught me. And worse, one of the hooded ones arrived to rap me with his glowing rod."

Sarah gasped.

And then her expression turned deadly serious.

"We can never travel apart again. We just can't! It's too dangerous." She paused in deep thought a moment.

23

"How long did it take them to find you?"

"Six days." Gordon thought a bit. "Yes, it was the sixth evening. I'd actually gotten a press pass to Princess Diana's wedding at St. Paul's Cathedral -- kind of spoiled that."

"Six days!" Sarah began tapping her foot impatiently.

"I know. They're finding us faster."

"It was only a few jumps back that we could stay for almost three weeks before they'd find us. Now, they can find us after only six days!"

"They're getting faster and better. And, it's getting harder to elude them once the chase has begun," Gordon said.

"That's why we came up with this plan, right?" Sarah smiled confidently. She nodded in answer to her own question. "Right. Well, we must be prepared beginning tonight, then."

"What?"

"Yes, tonight marks the sixth evening I've been here. We'll have to keep a sharp eye out once the sun sets."

Gordon and Sarah looked around at the lengthening shadows.

"Did you say Princess Diana's wedding? Back in the late twentieth century?" Sarah frowned in puzzlement.

"Yes."

"I was there once, I can almost remember it."

"Well, that would have been something if I had run into you, when you jumped in from a different time than when I left you here. I don't think we've managed that yet!" Gordon chuckled.

24

"Sounds a bit dodgy to me," Sarah whispered intently.

"And you were alone?"

"Yes, I was there at the cathedral. I remember her dress and that never-ending train distinctly. But, I was there alone. We don't time travel alone often ... " She rubbed her eyes tiredly as she tried to remember more. "Why would I have been there alone?"

Gordon thought a moment, his memories jumbled and confused in no apparent order. In one instant, he remembered being in the eighteenth century at a country wedding. And suddenly, his mind jumped to the twenty-second century ... and next a memory from the thirteenth century.

He closed his eyes and focused his thoughts.

He focused on time traveling alone ... memories of jumping from time to time ... There they were, he and Sarah ...

"We used to jump into a specific time separately for no more than forty-eight hours ... I remember that vaguely. We didn't want to be separated more than that. And, we were searching ... " Gordon felt the memory coalesce into certainty.

But in the next moment, the memory faded away.

"Yes ... yes! I remember that. But what were we searching for?" Sarah's blue eyes peered intently over the fields.

"We felt we had a better chance of finding it, if we jumped separately ... I remember that."

"It's so strange -- our memories are so diffused, like a fog. It's like my memories are all jumbled into such mixed up mess that ... that ... " Sarah choked back a sob.

"Now, now. Don't get worked up over it, darling. We've come to live with it, just as we have with being lost in time. We're a bit lost inside our heads as well, eh?"

"I hate it!" Sarah shouted.

And then she laid her head on his shoulder and cried.

"There, there." Gordon gently stroked her back. "You know, there is one thing I remember very plainly -- and it's part of every memory."

Sarah looked up, her tear-stained cheeks glistening.

"All my memories include you."

She smiled sweetly at him.

And as the birds serenaded them with their evening songs, Gordon held Sarah close and tenderly kissed her.

Sarah stepped back, and Gordon handed her a handkerchief from his coat pocket. She wiped her cheeks.

"Now, where is your Time Transporter?" Sarah asked.

"Right next to yours, per our plan."

"Great. Since they're so close, perhaps their sensors won't pick up that there are two, just as we hope. You'll need to hurry back after the last dance and start the final preparations. The Shadows will find me tonight -- it's my sixth night here. I feel sure of it."

"I will." Gordon suddenly broke out in a wide smile. "Something good did come out of my little skirmish."

"Really? What was that?"

"I got one of their glowing rods -- the one that gives off sparks!"

Sarah grasped his arm with pride.

"Excellent! Well then, that means our plan is one step ahead of the game already."

Gordon took out his watch. "We'd better get back."

And arm in arm, Gordon and Sarah walked back to the manor house.

They found Jane Austen standing near one end of the grand ballroom.

"Hello, Jane. Now, which lady and her partner are calling the dance tonight?" Sarah looked around at the gaily dressed couples with keen anticipation.

"My sister, Cassandra, and Mr. Cullens, her dance partner." Jane smiled mischievously.

"That name sounds so familiar!" Sarah's eyebrows rose inquisitively

"Oh, he's quite a character." Jane laughed knowingly. "There's no one else quite like him in the entire world I believe, if you gather my meaning!"

Sarah laughed hysterically a moment. "You know, I think I do. Oh, poor Cassandra!" Sarah chuckled.

Sarah and Jane laughed with delight.

"What dance shall be first tonight?" Gordon glanced around the ballroom. "Will it be a quadrille?"

"Oh, I wish it were a waltz," Sarah said wistfully.

27

"You astonish me!" Jane said in surprise. "The waltz is not danced here in England among gentle folk -- it's still considered quite controversial. I mean, men and women actually putting their arms around each other and holding themselves close while they dance."

"Oh dear," Gordon said in mock disapproval. "If we good English folk begin to allow waltzing, it could corrupt the moral fiber of our entire country. And, what would come next? Couples kissing and showing affection in plain sight!"

Sarah stifled a laugh as Jane Austen's eyes grew wide with shock.

"Mr. Smith, such an imagination!" Jane cried out. She flipped open her fan and waved it rapidly as if she were suddenly overheated.

Sarah laughed with unbridled joy when she caught Gordon's glance.

Gordon felt his heart stir with emotion.

"Mr. Smith and I have waltzed together many times in France," Sarah said proudly.

"Oh, my!" Jane fanned herself with more energy.

Gordon muffled a chuckle. The memories of many happy nights on the dance floor with Sarah in his arms came to mind. He looked deeply into Sarah's eyes.

"Yes, I love the feeling of holding a beautiful woman in my arms and guiding her around the dance floor." Gordon smiled knowingly.

Sarah chuckled with mirth.

Jane paused with her fan in mid-stroke as she glanced at Sarah.

"And I love the feeling of holding a handsome young man in my arms while he 'thinks' he's guiding me around the dance floor!"

Sarah and Jane laughed together at him.

Gordon took a deep breath, feigning perfect boredom with the present conversation, and looked away from Sarah and Jane -- two obviously overwrought young women -- and carefully observed some other couples happily chattering away.

"I wonder what dance shall be first?" Gordon asked again after a polite pause.

"Most likely, a typical English country dance," Jane replied as she finally managed to stop laughing.

Sarah wrapped her arm around Jane's arm.

At just that moment, Cassandra and Mr. Cullens stepped out of the crowd and waved for attention.

"Ladies and gentlemen," Cassandra said in a raised voice so all could hear. "Are you ready?"

A shout went up from all.

Cassandra raised her arms and called out loudly.

"Then, form a longwise set for as many as will!"

"Oh, this shall be fun," Sarah said excitedly.

The men formed a line on one side of the long ballroom while the ladies formed a line facing them.

Gordon stood before Jane Austen. Sarah was to dance with Major Wingart, a friend of Jane. Jane suddenly turned and whispered excitedly to Sarah.

Sarah's eyes sparkled at Gordon.

"Well, what mischief are you two whispering about now?" Gordon asked.

"Miss Austen wonders if you dance half as good

as you look!" Sarah laughed.

"Oh, Sarah!" Jane blushed brightly.

The music started, and all the gentlemen bowed to the line of beautiful ladies, who curtsied in polite reply.

The dance proceeded with a stately elegance combined with youthful exuberance.

Under the rows of flickering candles, the top couple stepped forward and joined hands. They gracefully danced a series of symmetrical figures as they moved down toward the end of the line while the other couples clapped and shouted approval. When they completed their final figure, the first couple stepped into their new places at the end of the line and joined the clapping and laughing while everyone looked up the line as a new couple stepped toward the center.

Gordon and Jane Austen stepped toward each other and bowed politely.

He smiled at Jane as they circled each other arm in arm, music and laughter filling the air.

"Isn't dancing great fun?" Jane laughed gaily as Gordon guided her in the simple circle.

"Lovely!" Gordon laughed.

And he meant it. It was fun.

Of course, he had to concentrate a bit more than most, since he didn't live in this century. He had done a quick review on the computer and practiced alone as he watched the dance figures performed on a video. He was very glad he had practiced now.

Still, actually performing the dance was an entirely different matter.

He felt a rising sense of panic when he and Jane

clasped hands and began the next figure in a counter-clockwise direction. He felt a sense of panic when he couldn't quite remember ...

Jane gently corrected him, and suddenly it came back to him. They quickly completed the figure and began the next as they eased toward the end of the rows of couples. Finally, they were dancing the last figure with only their fingertips touching.

He laughed out loud with relief when they skipped to the end of the line and finally finished.

Gordon felt a wave of relief as he and Jane Austen laughed at each other and stepped back into line.

They clapped and glanced back up as Sarah and Major Wingart danced their first figure.

Time melted into a joyous cacophony of laughter, music and gliding couples until the first of two sections of the dance came to its merry conclusion.

Cassandra called the first break, and all the dancers moved to different parts of the grand ballroom in order to rest before the second section of dances began.

Gordon, Sarah, Jane and Cassandra moved next to one of the large windows that looked out upon the darkened garden.

"My, how dark it is already," Cassandra exclaimed.

"A moonless night, tonight," Jane said in an overly dramatic tone. "A night in which one should not venture out alone -- as danger may lurk in those deep shadows..." Jane's eyes twinkled with mischievous delight.

Sarah locked eyes with Gordon.

"Oh, I didn't mean to scare you," Jane said immediately when she noticed their expressions.

"No, you didn't scare me. It's just, well ... " Sarah shrugged.

"You are staying the night here, as guest of the duke, right?" Jane took Sarah's arm. "My sister Cassandra and I are staying also. I thought you said you were too."

"Yes, I am." Sarah smiled.

"Then, you won't have to travel through the dreary darkness!"

"Though it is a beautiful house, I have never stayed here before. And, the prospect of sleeping in an unknown place the first time does make the heart nervous, does it not?"

"Indeed!" Cassandra agreed. "Yet, it is good you have us nearby in case you need comfort."

"Indeed, I am grateful you are so near." Sarah nodded politely.

"Then, I won't mention some of the stories I've heard about this house," Jane whispered mysteriously as Cassandra cast a disapproving expression.

"Oh, don't tell me it's haunted!" Gordon laughed.

"Enough of that talk," Cassandra admonished, taking Jane firmly by the arm. "We don't want to scare dear Sarah. She's already a bit nervous about sleeping here tonight."

"No, indeed. I do apologize, Sarah," Jane said sweetly.

"It's fine, Jane. You've not frightened me with

your words." Sarah smiled weakly.

"But, you are nervous about sleeping in this great house tonight?" Jane asked.

"Yes, I am a bit nervous about tonight." Sarah sighed

Chapter Three

Gordon hurried back to his Time Transporter after the last dance.

A light blazed out of the darkness as the door opened to his key. He stepped quickly inside and ran to the main console.

Dials, buttons and keyboards littered the entire left side of the Transporter. As his fingers danced over the controls with practiced precision, he glanced at the various screens.

Not that he could read them.

All the letters and words were in a kind of hieroglyphic gibberish that made absolutely no sense to Gordon. Even the controls bore labels in the same, unknown language.

That fact alone convinced both Sarah and Gordon that the Time Transporters were not made by humans.

But somehow, he knew exactly how to operate all the controls.

A whirlwind of emotions and questions flooded his mind again.

He couldn't remember how he'd learn to operate it. He couldn't remember the first time he traveled in it. He couldn't remember ... life before the Time Transporter.

In the kaleidoscope of jumbled memories that danced inside his mind in no apparent order, only two things were a constant -- Sarah and the Time Transporter.

He glanced across the room at the largest screen in the control room.

But, there was someone else: a mysterious voice and partly visible face that sometimes appeared briefly on that large screen and tried to communicate with them.

Unfortunately, the screen was broken. The voice and visage could only be heard in brief snippets at odd times. No real communication could take place -- only brief, tantalizing phrases and bits of messages.

If their plan worked tonight, perhaps they could make solid communication with this mysterious personage. And more importantly, maybe he could help answer some of their most pressing questions.

Gordon felt a slight queasiness in the pit of his stomach as the Transporter jumped through time and space.

It was the briefest of sensations, since he only jumped four hours forward in time and about three miles distance in space.

He grabbed a communicator and put several objects into his pockets before he slipped out the door and into the night.

"Sarah, are you there?" Gordon whispered into the microphone. He adjusted the earpiece on his left ear ever so slightly.

"Yes, I am sitting up in bed."

Gordon felt the adrenaline flowing through his veins with rising anticipation of the chase.

"Good. Have you heard anything?"

"Yes, the house is full of creaking noises."

"The Shadows are pressing between the boards and entering all the bedrooms," Gordon said, matter-of-factly.

"I know -- that always give me the creeps!" Sarah whispered urgently.

"Get your shoes on. It's almost time."

"I have them on already. And my housecoat too."

"Good. Wait until they sneak into the room with you."

Sarah groaned uncomfortably.

"Now, now, keep your chin up."

"Easy for you to say -- you're not the one about to get chased down dark halls by a horde of flying Shadows!"

"Put the band with the camera around your head and turn it on so I can see what you're seeing."

Gordon looked down at the miniature console he held in his hand and smiled as a picture appeared and resolved into a darkened bedroom.

"Good. I see your room," Gordon whispered.

Suddenly, a high-pitched creaking filled their ears, and both Gordon and Sarah tensed with adrenaline.

"It's coming inside now ... " Gordon whispered barely above a hush.

A loud pop reverberated inside the room.

"Now, run!"

***

Sarah jumped out of bed and bolted for the door. She threw it open and leapt into the darkened hallway.

And immediately, she was bowled over as a Shadow wrapped its tiny arms around her neck and shrieked with ghastly delight.

Sarah choked and gagged as its muscular grip

36

tightened. She heard the fluttering of more wings and realized at least two others would be on top of her in seconds.

She sat up and then fell backwards as hard as she could, right on top of the Shadow.

The tiny vise-like grip loosened.

She screamed as two more fluttered right above her, just over her face.

Sarah slapped them away with her hands and jumped back up on her feet and ran.

"They're too close!" Gordon whispered urgently.

"I know they're too close! Tell me something that can help me! Or else, just shut up!"

"You're going to have to take a detour."

"Right -- you've got that ready then?" Sarah said breathlessly.

"Yes, I scanned the house. There are two secret passages -- one is coming up at the room next to the top of the stairs."

"That's Jane's room!"

A leathery wing brushed against her face.

Sarah screamed and sent a fist into the almost invisible Shadow, throwing it against the wall with a thud.

"She'll be unconscious with a Shadow sitting over her and sucking her breath. She'll never know you're there."

"I hate that!" But with a renewed burst of energy, Sarah flung herself at the door. Fortunately, it was not locked.

Sarah burst into the room and shut the door immediately behind her.

She turned and found herself staring at a wide-awake and quite startled Jane Austen.

"My dear Sarah! What does this sudden intrusion mean?" Jane said with unbridled surprise as she stared at Sarah with wide eyes. "I was frozen in place listening to the ruckus outside and just about to get up when you burst inside. Are you in danger?"

Sarah noticed the two large candles and the open book before Jane. She knew immediately why the Shadows had not entered this room.

"There's no time for this," Gordon whispered with more urgency.

"Right," Sarah said out loud to both Gordon and Jane. "Where is it?"

"W-w-where is what?" Jane asked, dumbfounded.

"To the left of the bed should be a small board about waist level that you can swivel to reveal a latch -- get to it!"

Sarah ran toward the left side of the bed as Jane raised the covers to her face in fright.

"Sarah, you're scaring me!"

"Sssh!" Sarah ran her hands over the well-worn, ancient boards until she found one that moved slightly under her touch. She fumbled with it, trying to determine how to get it to move and reveal the latch.

Shrieks filled the air as the Shadows poured in around the edges of the bedroom door and into the lighted room.

Jane screamed with horror.

The candle to her right suddenly blew out as if by an invisible breath. A Shadow fluttered in the darkness, shrieking right next to Jane.

Jane screamed even louder.

The board gave way and moved to the side to reveal the latch. Sarah turned it, and a small door opened into a pitch-dark corridor beyond.

Sarah grabbed the lone candle with one hand and Jane's hand with her other. She couldn't bear the thought of the Shadows pinning Jane down and sucking her breath until she lost consciousness.

"Jane, we've got to run! Now!"

They both squeezed inside, and Sarah quickly shut the door. The edges were tight, but even as the door shut with a firm click, she heard the boards creaking and groaning violently as the Shadows fought to squeeze through.

"Run! The Shadows are coming for us!"

Jane and Sarah ran.

With the lone candle lighting the darkened corridor ahead for only a few feet, they ran as fast as they dared.

They coughed and swatted away cobwebs and screamed when unseen spiders just as startled as they were crawled down their arms.

More than once, Sarah ran into Jane and both stumbled to their knees.

Without warning, they came to a wooden wall.

Sarah turned around and glanced back down the dark corridor. In the complete darkness, she noticed movements in the darkness as the Shadows flew toward them.

"They're coming! What now -- we've run into a wall!"

"To your right, a latch should be right there,"

Gordon whispered.

Sarah handed the candle to Jane.

"Hold this up toward them. They're afraid of light. But hold it up so I can see over here too."

Jane's hand shook so badly she almost dropped the candle when Sarah handed it to her. She grasped it with both hands to keep from dropping it under the dire circumstances.

"I'm never going to sleep in any house ever again that is even whispered to be haunted!" Jane said.

"Right," Sarah said triumphantly as she found the latch in the flicking candlelight. She turned it, and the door opened inward into an empty bedroom.

Jane leapt through immediately. Sarah followed and shut the door firmly.

"Where to now?" Sarah whispered.

"Why ask me?" Jane cried out. "I surely don't know!"

"Ssssh," Sarah chided.

"You're in the farthest bedroom now. Run out the hallway door and down the servants' stairs to your immediate left," Gordon whispered into her earpiece as low as he could so Jane might not hear.

"I'm hearing voices now!" Jane looked all around the empty room. "I think I may be going mad!"

"Not quite yet." Sarah grabbed Jane by the hand and pulled her out into the hall.

They ran down the stairs two at a time and immediately ran though the empty kitchen and into the yard outside.

"We're out of the house now, just outside the

40

kitchen door."

Jane looked at her with shock.

"I know that, Sarah. You don't have to tell me, I'm right here!"

"Yes, I see it on the console," Gordon whispered.

"What's that whispering?" Jane cried.

Sarah shook her head and gestured for silence.

"Run around the lane beside the house and head for me. I'm right at the edge of the field waiting."

Jane's eyes widened at hearing the disembodied voice.

"He's a friend -- don't worry," Sarah said.

"An invisible friend? Shadows that fly? A haunted house!"

"No, it's just a normal, old manor house."

Jane stared at her.

"But you got the rest right."

Jane's mouth fell open

Sarah and Jane dashed outside through the door followed by a dozen Shadows that flew around them with a chorus of shrieks.

"Run!"

The two ran into the night and down the darkened lane toward the field beyond. The Shadows caught them quickly and began fly around their heads, reaching for them with their black talons.

Sarah and Jane waved their arms wildly. They heard the wing-beats all around and saw the talons reaching for them everywhere they turned.

A Shadow landed on Jane's back, and she screamed.

41

"Keep running!" Sarah shouted as two Shadows fell across her own shoulders.

"Almost ... " Gordon whispered.

Sarah and Jane kept running even as more Shadows landed on their backs and shrieked wildly, trying to force them down.

"Almost ... "

Sarah felt three more land on her back with their talons clawing through her clothes. All at once she stumbled under their growing weight. Beside her, Jane screamed and fell to the ground at the same time.

Sarah felt a wave of repulsion as she stared over at the Shadows writhing all over Jane's back and legs.

Sarah reached over to help. But she felt more and more Shadows crawling over her own back and holding her arms and legs down. In the next moment, she was face down on the grass. She felt them all over her now, shrieking and howling as their tiny talons pressed into her skin and pulled at her clothing.

Panic filled her heart when she realized she couldn't move.

She shuddered at each touch of their ice-cold talons.

"Close enough ... " Gordon whispered.

Chapter Four

Gordon's heart raced as he watched the console and heard Sarah's shuddering groans.

But he forced himself to wait. He had to wait until just the right moment.

"Gordon!" Sarah shouted.

"Oh, I forgot to tell you," Gordon whispered in a low voice so only Sarah could hear him in her earpiece.

"*What?*"

"I know what they want to do to us when they catch us."

Sarah groaned louder.

"Those glowing rods, the ones that give off sparks, are some kind of portable Time Transporter. They want to use them to send us on a one-way trip into time."

"*Now* you tell me!"

"Well, I thought you should know."

Gordon watched the console carefully, observing the picture being transmitted from the tiny camera attached to the band around Sarah's head. As he stared, he noticed movement off in the distant darkness.

"Hang on ... Here he comes ... "

Sarah groaned louder as she struggled even harder against the Shadows' grip.

Seconds later, faint footsteps drew closer.

Sarah stopped struggling.

Gordon and Sarah saw the dark outline of a cloaked and hooded figure staring down at her.

As they watched, he drew his right arm from

43

within the cloak and lifted up a glowing rod.

"We have you at last, Sarah Nightingale," the creature growled menacingly. "There will be no escape for you and your unfortunate friend, Jane Austen!"

The nightmare shape pulled back his black hood and revealed a silver face devoid of eyes, nose or mouth. He raised his glowing rod higher as sparks exploded in a shower and the air filled with electricity.

Jane Austen let out a sigh and passed out beside Sarah.

Suddenly, a bright light pierced the darkness.

Gordon stepped through the opened door that had appeared out of thin air. In a single movement, he tossed the omni-torch in the air.

The darkness surrounding the two fallen women lit up as if a huge spotlight had suddenly ignited.

The Shadows shrieked in pain and rose up in a huge flock of movement, flying off in every direction like bats leaving a cave at dusk.

The Anon dropped his rod and covered his featureless face. He bowed lower as he struggled to pull his hood back over his head to protect himself from the harsh light.

In two quick steps, Gordon retrieved the fallen rod and pointed it at the Anon.

Still bowed over on his knees with his cloak and hood over his head and shoulders, the Anon froze.

Sarah jumped to her feet.

"It worked!" Sarah shouted.

"It worked just like we planned!" Gordon laughed.

"But next time, you're the one that gets chased and caught while I call out the instructions from the Transporter!" Sarah said angrily. She shuddered. "Oh! I hate the feeling of their cold, clammy hands all over me!"

"But I think they like chasing you best, my dear."

Sarah shot him a look that could kill.

The Anon growled louder as the omni-torch fell to the ground and began to grow dim.

"Now, now old boy. Don't even think about running, or I'll use this handy rod to send you somewhere into time!" Gordon said with a deadly earnestness.

The Anon froze.

"Okay, Sarah, open the door. Once the light goes out, the Shadows will return."

"What about Jane?"

"You'll have to drag her in while I hold this thing at bay."

Sarah pulled at the leather choker around her neck and held a key up to the air before her.

An outline of bright light split the darkness as the door opened.

The Anon growled and stepped backwards.

"Hold still or I'll use this! I promise you that!"

A few moments later, Sarah dragged the unconscious Jane into the Time Transporter while Gordon held the rod at the Anon and forced him inside right behind them.

"Dim the lights, Sarah. I don't want him to panic."

Sarah worked the controls, and the lights

dimmed to half light.

"Well, it nearly worked to perfection." Sarah chuckled gleefully.

"Yes, they never noticed my Time Portal next to yours, just as we hoped."

"And when you moved it a short while ago, they remained focused on mine still in place."

"Yes, their sensors aren't as sensitive as they should be, eh." Gordon laughed.

"But, what will we to do about Jane Austen?" Sarah looked down at the unconscious figure.

"I'm thinking on it."

"What do you want from me?" the Anon asked with a deep growl.

At once, Sarah and Gordon focused on the faceless entity.

"You know something about this technology. I want you to make a repair for me," Gordon said carefully.

"Never!"

Gordon shoved the rod right up to the Anon's silver face.

He drew back in fear.

"I thought so. Well, if you don't do as I ask, I'll use this on you. I've already sent another of your kind on a one-way trip with one of these." Gordon reached over and picked up the other rod. He now pointed both at the awestruck Anon.

"I'll have no qualms about using both on you. No telling what that will do to you!"

"Please! Not both at once!" the Anon begged in a quavering voice.

"You'd never be found, would you?" Gordon

asked.

"I might not even survive."

"Well then, it's time for a deal. Are you game?" Gordon arched his eyebrows questioningly.

"I am listening."

"I will let you go -- minus this little toy -- if you do something for me, something quite simple for you, I believe."

"Proceed." He growled.

"I want you to repair this communication device over here." Gordon nodded to the corner where all the controls and displays were dark and silent.

The Anon growled.

Gordon held both rods right at its face.

"Put them down. I will do as you ask."

As Sarah and Gordon watched, the Anon pulled open the console and began poking around inside.

"What shall I do with Jane?" Sarah asked.

"Best to use a tranquilizer -- but it must be a special kind." Gordon paused in concentration. "Yes, one with some narcotic additives should do the trick. That will put her in a deep, deep slumber, and even when she awakens in the morning she'll feel disoriented for quite some time."

"Brilliant!" Sarah laughed. "When we put her back in bed, perhaps her thoughts will be so muddled she won't be able to distinguish between the real memories and the induced ones. She might not even remember all the events tonight, and what she does remember will be so mixed up with her drugged dreams ... "

"If Jane recalls any of the events clearly from tonight, it might cause a minor disruption of the

47

timeline." Gordon shook his head.

"Oh dear, just think how it might affect things if Jane Austen began to write horror novels instead of romance novels!"

"Yes, it's possible it could alter future history. We must do all we can to keep the timeline as pristine as possible."

Sarah walked down the hall toward a set of cabinets. She opened one and rummaged around until she found it. She quickly walked back and inserted the syringe into Jane's arm.

Jane sighed softly as she slipped deeper into unconsciousness.

"How's it coming?" Gordon asked the creature.

"It has been badly damaged. I can only do so much."

"You'd better do enough -- or else." Gordon pointed both rods at him.

A half hour passed slowly.

Finally, the Anon grunted with satisfaction.

"I have done all I can. You need to replace the main module; there are too many damaged circuits."

"Will it work now?" Gordon asked.

"For short periods. It will overheat and short out again. But, it will work for a few minutes at a time with my repairs."

"Let's try it." Gordon sat one of the rods down and used the other to force the Anon back against the wall while he stood before the control panel.

Once again, Gordon's heart raced -- but now, it raced with excitement.

"Oh Gordon, at last!" Sarah said excitedly.

Gordon stared at the blank screen.

As far back as his jumbled memories could remember, this communication console had been broken. And yet sometimes, once in a great while, it would come to life for a few brief seconds.

And in those brief moments, a face would appear.

The visage would try to communicate through the fog of static, but only a few words were ever discernable to either Gordon or Sarah.

But, one thing made them realize they desperately needed to communicate with this unknown entity.

It knew them by name.

"Go ahead, switch it on," Sarah urged him.

Gordon hesitated. Something inside made him fearful. It was almost as if he were afraid to finally learn the truth about this creature. As if knowing the truth might be worse than being lost in time and chased eternally by these nightmare creatures.

"Come on then, do it!" Sarah said firmly.

Gordon hit the power switch.

The display wavered as the console grew bright with activity.

"Well?" Sarah asked.

"Hang on -- it's been a long time."

Gordon stared at the unintelligible labels across the console. And yet he almost instinctively moved his hands over the buttons and dials as he tried to initiate contact.

It was as if he knew -- but he had no idea how he knew.

Suddenly, the face appeared on the display.

Sarah stepped beside Gordon as they stared in

hope and fear.

The round face was dominated by a short snout tipped with a small black nose with black lips underneath. The entire face was covered by short, jet-black fur. But its eyes were its most striking feature. The emerald-green eyes with dark, vertical pupils sparkled with intelligence.

Gordon noticed for the first time that the creature had six triangular-shaped ears -- two on top of its head, two on each side pointing outwards, and two located below its jaw and pointed downward at forty-five degree angles.

Gordon assumed it could hear quite well.

The creature smiled at him and then began to laugh.

"I knew you would fix it!"

Gordon stared at the creature.

"Who are you?" Gordon finally asked.

"You don't remember me?" the creature asked in surprise.

"No."

"Oh my -- that's not good." The creature's six ears stretched out with interest.

"Should I remember you?" Gordon leaned closer until his nose almost touched the screen.

"I remember you."

"Oh dear," Sarah whispered.

"Do you remember me, Sarah?" it asked.

"No, I don't."

The creature sighed and shook its head sadly.

"What does that mean?" Gordon prompted him.

"I'm not sure. But ... "

"But what?"

"I've never heard of this condition before." The furry-faced creature frowned.

"What is your name? Maybe if you tell us that, we'll remember you better," Sarah said excitedly.

"Ah, good idea, Sarah. You always did have excellent insights!" The creature smiled widely.

Sarah and Gordon looked at each other.

Gordon rolled his eyes. "Okay, then, let's have it already."

"Ah, yes. My name is Hylrada."

Gordon felt his heart skip a beat. He turned to Sarah.

"Yes, I know," she said, almost as if reading his own feelings. She gripped his arm firmly. "It sounds so familiar."

Gordon felt a wave of emotions rush through him. He tried to focus, to remember. But somehow, just out of reach of his consciousness was the answer.

He knew that name somehow. But, he couldn't quite remember ...

"Hylrada," Sarah repeated.

"Yes, did that help? Do you remember me now?" Hylrada asked excitedly.

"Sort of," Gordon replied.

Suddenly, the screen began to flicker. The acrid smell of burning circuitry grew discernable.

"Oh my, it seems as if your repairs are not sufficient," Hylrada said.

A bright light flashed behind them. They turned just in time to watch the Anon racing through the opened door and out into the darkness.

"Oh well, I was going to let him go anyway,"

Gordon said.

"Was that an Anon? Did he hear everything we said?" Hylrada asked in surprise.

"Well, yes. I forced him to make the repairs, actually." Gordon shrugged. "You see, I can work all the controls in the Transporter, but it's as if by instinct. I have no way to make repairs. I look inside at the circuits and my mind goes blank."

"Can't you read the manuals?" Hylrada asked with disbelief.

"No, it's all gibberish."

The screen flickered, and the burning smells increased.

"We need to end transmission. I will make contact again in exactly twenty-four hours. I'll run a quick remote test to see if there is more we can do on the repairs. And, we'll talk more."

"Wait, don't go. Not just yet," Gordon pleaded.

"We don't want to burn it out completely the first time, Gordon. There will be plenty more times we can chat," Hylrada purred.

"But, how do you know our names?"

"I have known both of you a long time." Hylrada smiled. "That's how I know your names."

"Why don't we know you then?" Sarah shouted. "I mean, I feel like I 'almost' know you, or remember you. But, I don't!"

She put her hands over her face in frustration.

"Let me ask you both a question."

Sarah and Gordon waited expectantly as Hylrada looked from one to the other.

"Do you remember your childhood? Do either of you remember your parents?"

Gordon felt dizzy. He swayed a moment and felt Sarah bump into him.

They looked at each other, and he realized she was just as disoriented as he felt.

"No, we don't," Gordon answered for both of them.

"I was afraid of that," Hylrada said. He paused a moment in thought. "I have a very important question to ask you now."

Gordon felt Sarah slip her hand into his hand. They held hands in frightened anticipation and mutual comfort.

"Do you recall any memories from before you began traveling through time?"

Gordon's racing heart beat even harder. He wanted to scream -- he wanted to cry out. He wanted to shout at Hylrada and put words to his burning confusion and mind-numbing frustration.

But before he could, Sarah replied in a surprisingly calm and emotionless voice.

"No, we don't. *And it frightens us.*"

Chapter Five

Gordon Smith yawned.

He hadn't slept well last night. He turned to Sarah, who smiled at him tiredly and quickly covered her own mouth as she yawned.

They both stood outside the manor house in the brisk, morning air.

"And what is it we're doing this morning?" Gordon asked.

"We're going out on a relaxing walk," Sarah replied cheerily as she adjusted her blue bonnet. She then smoothed out the flowing skirts of her blue plaid dress while humming a joyful tune. Finished with her tidying, she looked up at Gordon and smiled.

"A morning constitutional, is it?" Gordon asked.

"Well, if you're going to travel back in time and visit Jane Austen, there are two things one must absolutely do." Sarah chuckled and held up her forefinger. "First, one must attend a local ball -- which we did last night. And second ... "

"One must take a leisurely stroll in the country," Gordon finished for her.

"More than that, Gordon Smith -- much more than that."

Gordon held his walking stick close to his chest as he adjusted his top hat.

"And that is?"

"One must indulge in pleasant conversation. That, my dear Gordon, is the most important part of a walk in this day and age."

"Ha! I am an imbecile. How could I possibly

overlook that!" He chuckled with amusement as Sarah glanced around. The bright morning sun broke through the trees in bright rays of sunshine and revealed the natural beauty all around them.

Across the lane, Cassandra and Jane Austen emerged from the manor house. Each wore a bonnet on her head with a ribbon tied in a bow around her dainty neck. They held their long, flowing skirts up as they passed over the gravel drive and walked quickly towards Gordon and Sarah.

"I had imagined that reading one of her novels, if one traveled back in time to meet Jane Austen, would be a priority?" Gordon whispered as the two ladies approached.

"She's only published her first two novels up to this date. And neither bears her name as author. Each is listed as written 'By a Lady' right now."

Gordon suddenly felt a wave of dizziness again as his memories swirled with half-remembered visions.

"Funny how we can remember such details from history, and yet our personal history is such a total blank," Sarah said with a hint of sadness.

Gordon and Sarah looked deeply into each other's eyes with a pained yearning.

"There you are!" Jane said, a bit out of breath.

"I hope you have breakfasted. Walking without eating first can drain one so. Jane and I have just finished ours," Cassandra asked.

"Yes, we have. Thank you for your concern," Sarah said.

"Then, let us walk while the birds serenade us with their joyous, morning chorus." Jane's eyes twinkled happily.

The four walked a while in contented silence as the birds indeed sang to them from seemingly every tree branch. After they had passed a field of waving grass and then walked along a forest path for quite some time, Jane finally spoke.

"I had the strangest dreams last night."

Gordon and Sarah stopped in mid-step and stared at Jane with questioning expressions.

"Oh, look how concerned they are for you, dear sister," Cassandra said approvingly.

"It's just that, well, I must confess that I too had some strange dreams last night." Sarah grasped Jane tenderly by her arm.

"What were these strange dreams?" Gordon used his walking stick to push up the brim of his top hat.

"They were most alarming, and yet ... yet I only recall bits and pieces amid a deep fog of fear." Jane shook her head emphatically.

"You can recall nothing of substance?" Gordon asked with a hint of hope.

"I seem to recall bats." Jane's eyes narrowed in deep thought. "Yes, very large and very frightful bats. And they were chasing me. And try as I might, I could never quite escape them no matter how fast I ran. It was terrifying!"

"Oh, I hate those kinds of nightmares," Cassandra added sympathetically.

"One has only to awaken and such frightful images are gone with reality." Gordon snapped his fingers to emphasize his point.

"Ah, but there was another figure -- a terrible,

56

dark figure covered with a black cloak and hood."

Gordon and Sarah both went still as they waited for Jane's next words.

"And most frightening of all, he had no face!"

"No face!" Cassandra put her hands to her cheeks in shock.

"How could someone not have a face?" Sarah prompted.

"I don't know. But, it gives me shivers just thinking about it." Jane put her arms around her waist as if hugging herself for comfort.

"Well, it was just a nightmare. The beautiful scene around us must push such momentary images out of our minds -- never to be remembered again." Gordon smiled confidently.

"Mr. Smith is quite right, dear Jane," Cassandra said soothingly as she put her arm around Jane's shoulders. "One must put away the fantasies of the night and revel in the beauty of reality around us now."

"Yes, the golden daylight must forever push the fearful night away with each sunrise. Let us enjoy our walk." Sarah started forward.

"I fear the manor house must indeed be haunted. I don't see how I could ever sleep there again."

Jane's words caused Sarah to freeze again. She turned.

"Now, now. Your feelings get the better of you, Jane. Don't let this matter cause you undue concern," Sarah advised politely.

A mischievous smile lit up Jane's face.

"But, I think I may use these dark and foreboding feelings to advantage."

"How could you possibly do that, dear sister?" Cassandra asked with puzzlement.

"I shall use the fear of a haunted house in my next story. I will create a small sub-plot within the overall story."

Gordon felt Sarah's hand grip him hard.

"What's the matter?" he whispered so only Sarah could hear him.

Cassandra and Jane walked ahead arm in arm. Sarah held Gordon back until the two sisters had walked several paces ahead. As they continued, Gordon heard Jane talking excitedly to Cassandra about a new story she was writing.

"I hope we haven't tampered with the timeline!" Sarah whispered urgently.

"What, Jane Austen is going to write a horror novel now and change the world?" Gordon asked playfully.

"No, not that!"

"Then, what?"

Sarah gripped his arm so tightly it actually became painful. She leaned close to him and whispered anxiously, "She does use a haunted house as a plot device in her novel *Northanger Abbey*."

"So, what's the problem? We simply inspired her." Gordon chuckled.

"How could we ever be her inspiration? We're not of this time! We're not even supposed to be here!" Sarah whispered.

"As long as she doesn't add huge flying bats and a cloaked figure with no face to her story, I don't see a problem." Gordon nodded reassuringly.

Sarah shook her head nervously. "I guess. It's

just, oh ... I just don't feel comfortable about it. I mean, what if we have changed history in some subtle way. How can we know? We may have started a small but significant chain of events that may alter history as we know it!"

"Sarah, I think you're going a bit overboard. The poor girl just had a bad dream. Yes, the giant, flying bats were real -- sort of -- in that they were half-seen flying Shadows. Yes, the faceless and hooded figure that scared the wits out of her last night was also real. And yes, Jane Austen came within moments of being tossed out of this time period and forced to live the rest of her life ... somewhere else. But other than that, it's wasn't that bad." Gordon patted Sarah's shoulder. "And with the medication, she only recalls bits and pieces and thinks it a mere nightmare now."

Sarah punched Gordon on the arm -- the same arm as last night.

"Ow! You've given me a bruise there, I believe." Gordon stepped away from her.

"Don't make fun of me," Sarah said with serious tone.

"All right. But, you're taking this too far."

"But, what if she was meant to get this idea of a haunted house months from now, and from an entirely different source?"

"I don't know. Perhaps we ought to ask our new friend tonight -- the furry fellow with six ears."

"He frightened me," Sarah said.

"It frightened me because he seemed so familiar and yet at the same time so ... so ... "

"So unfamiliar." Sarah looked at him with an

59

expression of deep concern.

"We'll figure it out. And look on the bright side -- the first part of our plan worked! We got that communication console fixed at last." Gordon smiled proudly.

"Yes, that is something." Sarah wrapped her arm inside Gordon's arm, and they slowly began to walk together.

Up ahead, Cassandra and Jane were walking leisurely while totally immersed in their own private conversation.

"I am so afraid sometimes."

Gordon gently patted Sarah's hand. "Last night was our first step out of this nightmare, Sarah. We finally did something different. It seems we've been running from the Shadows and the Anon forever. But last night, we finally fought back."

"How long have we been running?" Sarah's voice trembled with emotion.

"I don't know. My recent memories are just a jumble -- one chase after another, one time after another. It's all I can remember. Whether it's been months or years or decades, I can't tell." Gordon took a deep breath.

"And, how do we know how to operate the Time Transporters? We can't even read the labels on the controls!" Sarah said breathlessly.

"It's as if the knowledge is burned inside my mind, somehow. I don't have any distinct memories of training or learning to use it. I just ... *know*." Gordon slowly shook his head.

"Perhaps Hylrada can tell us?" Sarah asked hopefully.

"That is my hope as well. After all ... "

Sarah eye's widened with anticipation as she waited for his next words.

"He knows us. And more important, he remembers us ... "

Chapter Six

"I can't tell you about your past until I understand what happened to cause your bizarre memory loss. It might not be safe for you. We must be careful."

Hylrada looked at them in contemplative silence.

"But, you knew us before we lost our memory -- before we were lost in time?" Gordon asked.

"When I met you, you were being pursued by a very powerful and a very terrible enemy. You were traveling through time then just as you are now."

"But not by the Shadows? Or the cloaked figures who call themselves Anon?" Gordon waited impatiently as he stared at the visage on the communication console.

"The Anon are bounty hunters. The Shadows are their hounds. They pale in comparison to the evil that was pursuing you when we first met."

"How long ago was that?" Sarah asked. "I mean, I assume you have remained in your time period and can tell us in years?"

"You're obviously not human though. Do you even count time in years?" Gordon shot back.

"I have studied Earth and humans all my life, so I am familiar with your kind and your measurements. And you are right -- I'm not human. I am Alfrian. My home world exists on the entire opposite side of the galaxy from Earth."

"I don't recall in any part of Earth history where we meet aliens." Sarah asked.

"No, not until far into the future in real

space/time. But within the ether outside space/time, aliens have visited Earth at many points in your timeline."

"And that's how you met us?"

Hylrada looked from Gordon to Sarah. "I will travel into time to enhance my research, but only when absolutely necessary. However, I first contacted you via remote communications just like we're talking now, after my temporal sensors detected your time machine."

"So, how long have you known us?" Gordon asked.

"I met you five years ago -- in actual space/time and based on Earth's orbit. You needed my help then, just as you need it now."

"How did you help us the first time?" Gordon tapped his fingers impatiently.

"I gave you the Time Transporters."

"And you taught us to use them?" Sarah bent close to the console with eager expectation.

"We didn't have time -- your lives were in danger and you needed to travel into time immediately in order to escape." Hylrada swallowed nervously and continued. "And so, I took a shortcut."

"Shortcut?" Gordon and Sarah asked simultaneously.

"I used a device to implant the training inside your minds. Ah, how can I explain it -- you don't have such technology on Earth. At least not until after the twenty-eighth century."

"It burns the knowledge into our synapses?" Sarah suggested.

63

"That is too simple an explanation for the process -- and yet it explains the concept adequately."

"It's more of a chemical process," Gordon guessed.

"Electro-chemical, yes," Hylrada replied.

Gordon and Sarah exchanged glances.

"And what about this enemy?"

"We must be careful with this link; the console signal is steadily growing weaker even as we speak, and we can't afford to allow it to fail totally and cut us off again." Hylrada began typing on an unseen keyboard.

"I am sending you instructions on how to make the repairs more satisfactory and allow the console to function for longer periods." Hylrada typed furiously.

"I hope it's in English!"

"Of course." Hylrada stopped typing and looked up at them. "Make the repairs per these instructions. Also, you cannot stay in that time any longer; the Shadows have already sniffed you out and no doubt are waiting to follow you to where you will sleep and then attack again."

"Sarah's Transport is right beside mine. She'll be out and inside it within three steps and we can both jump." Gordon looked over at his Sarah.

She smiled at him. Her sad eyes sparkled with eagerness as she ran her hand through her sandy blonde hair.

"Right. You must decide on a time so I can tune my communicator."

"Let's visit Paris, April tenth, the year 1924. Ah,

spring time in the 'City of Light.'" Gordon closed his eyes and smiled.

"Street cafes, wine and evening strolls by the Seine," Sarah added eagerly.

"You must be careful not to contaminate the timeline," Hylrada said with a deadly serious tone.

"We're too busy being chased to do that." Sarah sighed. "At least, intentionally."

"Do you recall the dangers inherent with time travel?"

"We don't even remember the first time we traveled through time." Gordon shook his head.

"Which brings us back to the really important mystery -- what do you remember?" Hylrada's six ears perked up with interest.

"Jumping through time and being relentlessly chased." Gordon chuckled. "We do recall important individuals of history, especially those that interest us. And I remember significant events clearly – wars, discoveries, catastrophes and such."

"Such as?" Hylrada asked.

"I know Mozart's music and am familiar with his life and the time period he lived. And I know a lot about Leonardo da Vinci and his fantastic accomplishments." Gordon smiled.

"You should be able to recall some of the history of your timeline then -- you remember the time of historical figures as well as Sarah's beloved Jane Austen."

"Yes." Sarah's tone was matter of fact. "It's strange, but we do have extensive memories of Earth's history and ancient time periods -- famous people, important places and historic events. It's like our general memories are all intact -- just our personal memories are missing."

"Do you think our memory loss is accidental or premeditated?" Gordon asked.

Sarah's eyes widened with interest.

"I am not sure at this point. Could it be accidental? Perhaps you've broken a fundamental law of physics in one of your time travels? That is possible -- for instance, what if you traveled back to the same point in space/time several times and met yourself coming and going? That could be very bad. One must exercise care in traveling through time."

Sarah took a deep breath.

"Now, could it be premeditated -- perhaps you were drugged and it caused your amnesia? That is possible, though most drugs would also cause severe emotional and mental side-effects as well. Until I observe you more, I cannot say." Hylrada sat back in his chair and shrugged. "Could the terrible enemy I mentioned when I first met you have caused this? He is utterly evil, and I would not put such a deed beyond him. He is a genius, though warped by his evil. He could have trapped you in some exotic stratagem. But, if he was the cause, what exactly did he do? I have no way to know until I make more observations and dig deeper into the anomalies of time travel that might create such a condition."

Hylrada pressed his face closer until his eyes and nose filled the entire screen. "I hope for your sakes he was not the cause of this amnesia."

"Tell us more about him. Why is he so evil? Why was he chasing us?" Sarah asked with a sudden eagerness.

"Not just yet. But I will tell you -- soon."

"I hate it!" Gordon stood up and began pacing the floor. "It feels like someone took a food blender and stuck it inside my head and turned it on high until all my memories were either scrambled or completely destroyed!"

"Calm yourself, Gordon. I am here once again. I am your friend and Sarah's friend. I will do all in my power to help you both." Hylrada smiled broadly.

"I trust you," Sarah said simply. "I'm not exactly sure why, but I trust you."

Gordon nodded in agreement but remained silent with his emotions boiling.

"And nothing of your childhood? Or any memory from prior to time traveling?"

"Nothing."

"That is very odd," Hylrada mused out loud.

"We're a bit surprised that we haven't met other humans traveling through time," Gordon interjected.

"No surprise there," Hylrada said confidently.

"Why do you say that?" Sarah asked.

"I've studied your world and the rise and fall of Earth's civilization, which span over fifty millennia of your history. Of course, there are literally thousands of times humankind experimented with time travel. And yet, you are the only two humans I have ever met who have accomplished it. In fact, I've never come across any publications from Earth that mentions a team successfully sending humans through time." Hylrada shook his head with bewilderment.

"Surely, some of the experiments were successful," Gordon said.

"At least one of them!" Sarah added quickly.

"That's the thing with traveling through time." Hylrada again leaned forward until only his emerald eyes and the tip of his black nose filled the screen. "First, the physics that make time travel possible are practically incomprehensible to creatures of the normal space/time continuum. Scientists trying to grasp the concept alone have difficulty. They literally have to think outside the universe and the laws that govern its existence. And to understand in detail the bizarre mathematics that define the ether and the ability to travel through time, equations that don't even exist inside space/time but exist solely outside it -- and then discern the infinite complexities and fantastical formulas and use them to construct a working device that can escape a universe bound by 'normal' physics and travel through time ... It's -- well -- almost unthinkable."

"Not just think outside the box -- think outside the entire universe. How could someone wrap their head around that?" Sarah rolled her eyes with amazement.

"And not go insane in the process," Gordon added with a hint of incredulity.

"How could anyone ever come up with it then?" Sarah asked.

"It would be almost impossible." Hylrada took a deep breath. "Unless such creatures were helped by those who themselves live outside the universe."

"The Anon!" Gordon said enthusiastically.

"Perhaps ... or others even more adept. But why

would they help others travel into their domain and give them the ability to jump to any point in the timeline?" Hylrada sat back and continued speaking.

"And so we come to the dangers involved when creatures leave the 'normal' universe and travel through the ether outside space/time and reenter space/time at a completely different point from their existence. The dangers this could cause to the timeline are almost as infinite as the possibilities -- but the potential dangers to the individuals are no less so."

Sarah crossed her arms confidently. "You yourself said you met us traveling through time. Did we mention any scientists by name on the project team? Or the year we succeeded?"

"Good questions." Hylrada leaned back and fell back into his chair. "I will need to check my notes. I recall that both of you were quite confident in your abilities to traverse time with the time machine you originally used. It was, of course, of human origin. And, I do seem to recall one of you mentioning the project -- but nothing concrete comes to my mind, and that in itself is a bit odd."

"We don't want you to lose your mind like us!" Gordon laughed.

"I certainly don't recall either of you complaining of memory loss at the time. I do recall something about your mission ... a very important mission."

"We don't even recall that little bit," Gordon said.

"Strange." Hylrada stroked his furry chin.

"Do your people travel through time often?" Sarah asked.

"Very, very rarely -- mainly for research. Dangerous stuff -- traveling through time. Not for the fainthearted, you know."

Gordon and Sarah exchanged surprised glances.

"The Anon must travel through time a lot."

"They live among the ether outside the space/time continuum. Actually, they rarely appear inside space/time. Their race is very old and very powerful."

"So, they live outside our universe." Gordon whistled in surprise.

"And the Shadows?" Sarah asked.

"They live within the ether as well, outside space and time. Bizarre creatures, those Shadows -- nasty buggers. They are not self-aware entities -- more like animals. You don't want them to catch you while not on the leash of an Anon. It could be ... fatal."

Gordon saw Sarah shudder with repulsion.

"How are we the only humans to ever travel through time?" Gordon asked. "You said that scientists experimented with it all through Earth's history."

"I've often wondered that. I wanted to question you about it further. But, in all the frantic activity of your pursuit, we never had time to discuss it in detail. It was all I could do to keep you one step ahead of him. And suddenly, I could no longer communicate with you at all -- until now."

"Who was this enemy chasing us back then?" Gordon felt his heart racing with adrenaline. Merely the mention of it sent him into a hurricane of emotions.

"Soon. I am afraid to tell you more in your present condition."

"And what are the dangers in time traveling -- so we can avoid them?" Sarah asked.

"The first is obvious -- you wouldn't want to meet yourself. You must recall the normal universe is a place of balance -- from the atomic level up to the astronomical level -- a place of order and balance.

"Oh, it's not so bad if an older version meets a younger version -- briefly. But, if you travel back to a point in space/time and meet yourself when you are close to the same age -- physically -- it would upset the delicate balance of nature. Really, the results are unpredictable, but the implications are enormous. Just imagine if suddenly there appeared another Earth within close proximity to the original Earth! The gravity well would be completely changed; the fabric of space/time would be greatly disturbed. Such an event would be catastrophic for both planets.

"Now, imagine that you and a second version of yourself appeared simultaneously at almost the same spot in space and time. Meeting yourself ... one version maybe only a few moments younger than the other -- each unique entity suddenly in the same place at the same time. Well, I wouldn't recommend it."

"Do you think that's what happened to us? Perhaps that's why our memories are so fragmented and damaged?" Sarah pressed her hand over her mouth in fright.

"I don't know."

"But, we're different than when you knew us before," Gordon said.

"Something has ... changed. You and Sarah are ... changed. You both seem strangely different from the Gordon and Sarah I helped all those years ago."

"Can you help us find our past? Can you help us remember who we were and how we got here? Can you help us find our way back?" Sarah cried out.

"Ever since I met you, I've been searching for the project and the scientists that succeeded in its efforts to travel through time. It should be a significant milestone in one age of Earth's history. That success should be plainly recorded. And when I find it, I should find you -- the two people they sent into time."

"And have you found anything? Any hint at all?"

"Nothing ... "

72

Chapter Seven

"There is a disturbance in the timeline around Earth."

Gordon looked up at the screen.

He and Sarah had just returned from a leisurely dinner at a Parisian street café near their parked Transporters. They had been in Paris circa 1924 for three days now, and the problems about missing memories, Shadows and other such nonsense had been pushed into the background as they enjoyed the many delights of the City of Lights. They were just getting acquainted with a bottle of good French wine when Hylrada's words diverted their attention.

"What kind of disturbance?" Sarah sipped her glass of wine.

"The anomaly is faint. But what makes it so dangerous is that it has appeared at a crucial juncture in Earth's history." Hylrada nodded.

"What do you mean?" Gordon asked.

"There are many important crossroads in the timeline. Some are decisive battles that determine how history will unfold in one direction or another. But, some of the most important junctures -- and the most fragile -- hinge on the history of a single individual. These individuals are unique throughout the history of any race and any culture. They may be called a genius, or a prophet, or an artist. But no matter, the heritage of this individual lives on generation after generation -- their work or their art or their thoughts living on through time and influencing entire populations for millennia."

"What makes the timeline so fragile?"

"If some malevolent force wants to tamper with an entire population of a planet, subtly changing the history of such an individual whose influence ripples through time like a tidal wave can make that possible with minimum effort." Hylrada pointed his finger at them. "Perhaps simply changing a single event in that person's life -- a setback at a key moment in their career that not only changes their life course but also that of history afterward."

"You're scaring me now," Sarah said.

"Isn't there some kind of control or some kind of temporal police to make sure these kinds of things don't happen?" Gordon asked.

"Yes indeed, such a Temporal Authority is much needed. I only wish ... well, never mind." Hylrada paused in thought. "As a matter of fact, one of my capacities is that of a scientific consultant to detect and report such temporal transgressions so that they may be prevented. However, most temporal changes that could affect an entire planet are easy to detect and subsequently to prevent. The kind I just described -- well, I'm not even sure there is an actual problem, and so I cannot engage the, um, Temporal Authorities officially at this time. But, I don't like the looks of it, and I feel it should be investigated."

"Then why tell us?" Sarah glanced at Gordon, who nodded in agreement with her.

"Because it is your world. You are its only time travelers, the only humans in a position to investigate further. Because you are human, you could look around and probably not raise any kind of suspicion -- even if I am wrong."

74

"Sounds reasonable," Gordon agreed.

"Most important, I know how much you care. I know you'll leave no stone unturned." Hylrada purred.

"What time period are we talking about? And, who is the individual?" Gordon sat up straight in anticipation.

"The year is 1598. The month is December. The place is London." Hylrada paused.

"And the individual is William Shakespeare," Sarah added without hesitation.

"Wow!" Gordon said, his excitement reverberating throughout the room.

"What's so crucial about that year? Hasn't Shakespeare hit the big time by then?" Sarah asked.

"The Lord Chamberlain's Men, Shakespeare's acting company, have indeed played before the queen and the royal court several times already. However, many people in key positions have taken a dislike to actors and plays and especially to certain playwrights. Some feel that they are corrupting the population's morals, possibly fomenting rebellion and definitely capable of influencing the entire city with subtle messages embedded within their plays."

"Sounds like that could be a slight problem."

"Throw in outbreaks of the plague and the threats of rebellion within the country and outright rebellion next door in Ireland, and you have quite a volatile atmosphere. And yet, it is worse for Shakespeare. Their home theater located in Shoreditch is empty; they have not been able to act on its stage in almost two years. And without a home -- without an audience -- how can a playwright and his actors survive?"

"What's happened with that?"

"The lease has expired and the owner has succumbed to public pressure to close down the theater because of its supposed corrupting influence. Now, he is going to tear down the theater and sell the wood as scrap."

"I thought Shakespeare's plays were performed at the Globe Theater south of the Thames?" Sarah asked. "I'm sure that was it."

"During the last week of December, William Shakespeare, Richard Burbage, Will Kempe and the rest of the troupe will lead a bold and truly desperate act. They will hire a carpenter and workmen and march along with them carrying the very weapons they use in their plays. They will march into Shoreditch and disassemble the entire theater within a few days and carry the timbers to a new location and begin constructing the Globe Theater. It is at this point in his life that Shakespeare elevates his genius by writing and performing what are considered his greatest plays."

"So, if he doesn't build the Globe ... he never writes those plays?"

"*Julius Caesar*, *As You Like It*, *Henry V*, *Hamlet*, *Macbeth* and many others ... lost forever." Hylrada sat back with a forlorn sigh.

"What can we do?" Sarah jumped up, ready for action.

"You and Gordon need to travel back and meet Shakespeare and determine if this anomaly is indeed a premeditated attempt to change Earth's history -- and prevent it!"

"No pressure there." Gordon chuckled.

"I have worse news." Hylrada sat back with a serious expression and slowly looked from Gordon back to Sarah.

"Don't leave us hanging," Gordon said.

"There is a signature, a faint one, of a Time Transporter. I've seen it before. It is the one used by that dreaded enemy I mentioned before -- the one who was chasing you when I first met you."

"What is his name?" Sarah asked. "We need to know that, if we are to face him."

"His name is ... Dragnorr!"

Chapter Eight

"London is crowded and noisy no matter the century."

Gordon glanced around at the throngs of people walking up and down West Cheap just below Guildhall. The streets were packed even in the midst of winter -- everyone trudging along bundled up with scarves, hats and heavy coats of every description.

"The pub is two blocks up from here," Sarah said confidently.

"Hylrada certainly has a way about him. He's provided us with every detail we need here -- money, maps, clothing and a list of helpful information." Gordon rubbed his hands together to warm them against the cold December air.

"I've got a letter of introduction that entitles me to start work as a barmaid at the pub too! Hylrada knows his stuff." Sarah waved the sealed envelope.

"The Three-legged Dog." Gordon looked up the street until he spotted the very sign with that title along with a picture of the unique canine.

"Shakespeare's favorite hangout." Sarah laughed.

"Favorite pub for most of his troupe," Gordon added. He suddenly paused as a thought struck him.

"Ever since Hylrada told us Dragnorr's name, I keep having these weird flashbacks. It's like I can almost see him -- but it's always out of focus. Yet, I'm certain I've seen him before. And now, we're going to face him -- again. But, I don't feel ready! It creeps me out," Gordon said with a concerned expression.

"Yes, I'm experiencing that too." Sarah rubbed her arms vigorously. "It was odd too. Hylrada's reports provided us with a lot of information. And yet, he didn't have a single picture of him."

"Right. He told us how he operates, he showed us Dragnorr's long list of crimes -- but it's almost like Dragnorr is invisible." Gordon rubbed his face.

"It's a strange feeling." Sarah's expression filled with deep concern.

"And, I'm sure -- somehow -- that we have unfinished business with him. We have fought him before, but our memories of him ... are shattered. It puts us at a dangerous disadvantage. I just hope we're truly ready when it comes time for the final showdown." Gordon shook his head.

"Listen, Hylrada prepared us well. He wouldn't have sent us out here unless he felt we were ready." Sarah smiled confidently. "He also equipped us for almost any eventuality. We'll make our reports to him every night from our Time Transporters. And if things get too hot, he said he would send in backup."

"True." But Gordon's tone was anything but confident.

Sarah grabbed Gordon's coat sleeve. "Best of all, we're going to meet William Shakespeare in a few minutes. Doesn't that excite you?"

"Yes, it does."

"Then stop worrying! I trust Hylrada. He'll be there if we need him."

"That's true. But -- "

"Look! There's the alley where we should find

young Tom Walker. Let's go." Sarah crossed the street between two wagons stopped at an intersection.

Gordon trotted along behind her. They trekked through the maze of pedestrians until they found the small alley behind a clock shop. As he looked down, he saw a number of scruffy-looking children playing.

"Hello!" Gordon shouted to them. "Which one of you is Tom Walker?"

"Who's asking?"

The tallest boy, and the only one with ebony skin, peered intently at them..

"I'm Gordon Smith. I was told that Tom Walker was the best runner in London."

The boy's dirt-covered face lit up with a smile.

"That's me, all right," he replied cheerfully.

Tom stepped closer. He ran his fingers through his short black hair as he studied Gordon and Sarah with his brown eyes. And though he was but a youth, the determined expression on his handsome face hinted at an inner strength far beyond his years.

Gordon rubbed his chin as he looked him up and down. "Do you know the streets of London, Tom?"

"Yes, sir!" Tom laughed. "Born here, I was."

"Ah, and you've got the accent to prove it." Gordon smiled.

"What's the job?" Tom crossed his arms.

"Well, then." Gordon reached inside his pocket and pulled out a half crown. He held it up plain to see.

Tom Walker stared at the coin intently.

"This is to hire you." He flipped the coin in the

air. Tom caught it easily with one hand. He rubbed it a moment and quickly put it deep in his pocket.

"Right! What do you want me to run?"

"You know a man named William Shakespeare?"

"Yes, sir. I know him by sight."

"Good, I thought you might. I need you to keep an eye on him the next few nights. Follow him, but don't let him know you're following him."

Tom waved his hands confidently. "I can follow anyone around London and they never know I'm there, mate!"

"Right. Well, there's a bit more. I think someone else is following him. So, you'll have to spot this fellow without him realizing you're there. Think you can handle that?"

Tom nodded. "Sure. But, how many nights you need me to do this?" He pulled the coin out and flipped it in the air and caught it again. "I mean, this might do for one night's work."

Gordon and Sarah exchanged smiling glances.

"There's one of those for each night's work -- after you've done the job. You only get this one up front so you know I'm on the level." Gordon reached out and tousled the boy's hair in a friendly manner.

Tom threw his head back and smiled. He glanced at Sarah and whistled appreciatively. "I say, she's pretty. Is she your wife?"

Sarah turned to Gordon with eyebrows raised and a twinkle in her blue eyes. And with a big smile, she opened her parasol and walked around Gordon, humming gaily.

81

Gordon almost felt nervous -- but he knew Sarah was playing with him after the lad had opened the door for her so easily.

"Well, I've not gotten around to anything so permanent quite yet. You see, I just haven't found the right *time*!"

Sarah laughed out loud and cast a knowing glance at him.

Gordon chuckled and reached out and took her arm. He started to walk off with her back up to the main street filled with pedestrians.

"Hold on, sir! How will I find you?" Tom called.

"We'll be at the 'Three-legged Dog' each night. You can report to me there and get your next coin."

"I have a question for him before we go." Sarah paused in thought a moment and then spoke. "Have you seen a newcomer around master Shakespeare or any of his friends lately?"

"Oh yes, and you can't miss him either."

"What do you mean?" Sarah asked.

"He's got dark skin, like me. And, he's a great, big bloke too." Tom slapped his thigh with a laugh.

"Is he an actor?" Gordon asked.

"I'm not sure. But ..." Tom motioned for them to come closer so he could say the next privately. "To tell you straight, there's something different about him -- not quite right, if you know what I mean."

"Uh, what do you mean?" Gordon rubbed his chin.

"I can't put my finger on it. I guess you'll just have to see for yourself." Tom nodded.

Gordon and Sarah turned again for the main street.

"Wait up -- what if something happens later when I follow him?" Tom put his hands on his hips.

Gordon and Sarah stopped. Gordon loosed his arm from Sarah's and walked back. He bent over until he was eye level with Tom.

"First thing, this man that we think is following Mr. Shakespeare -- he's a bad lot. Don't let him get his hands on you." Gordon held his forefinger up for emphasis.

"He won't even know I'm there!" Tom replied boldly. "And no one can catch me in a flat-out run, if it comes to that!"

"Good, lad." Gordon patted the boy on his shoulder. "But, if something happens late, you know the street Shakespeare lives on just off Bishopsgate?"

"Yes, sir!"

"There's a little alley just past his house. You just come running up that alley and whistle out loud. I'll see you."

"What?" Tom asked, appearing quite baffled as he looked at Gordon's fashionable clothes. "You live in an alley?"

"Just do as you're told, lad. Come to the alley even if it's late at night -- I'll see you."

"Right!"

"Now then, Miss Sarah and I are now going to the aforementioned pub and drink a few pints with Mr. Shakespeare." Gordon stood up and waited.

"I'll be outside waiting when he leaves, sir."

"Good, lad."

Gordon walked up to Sarah, who offered her arm.

"I think it's time we met this fellow Shakespeare, don't you think, my dear?" Gordon asked cheerfully.

"Indeed, Mr. Smith. Indeed, I do!"

Chapter Nine

The sign over the busy pub had a green background with a bold Dalmatian dog standing at the ready with his left hind leg attached to a peg leg and a red scarf around his neck.

Gordon waited outside discreetly as Sarah walked inside to present her letter of employment. He glanced up and down at the bustling throngs on High Street midway between Bishopsgate and Shoreditch.

As he waited, he felt a thrill of excitement. The intense feeling almost chased the cold out of the frigid London air.

He smiled broadly as he contemplated meeting William Shakespeare.

Gordon realized he had too much energy to merely wait. He walked briskly north a few blocks to take a peek at 'The Theater.' A few minutes later, he turned down Holywell Lane. He stopped suddenly in mid-step. The famous wooden structure rose out of the darkness with a strangely surreal quality.

He breathed deeply as he looked it over.

"Well, if history goes right, you'll be taken apart timber by timber next week and rebuilt into the most famous theater the world has ever known just south of the Thames," Gordon whispered as his misty breath drifted above his head.

He strolled around the strangely silent structure and took it all in a few minutes. Finally, he turned and walked back to the pub.

Gordon walked inside and was greeted by a

cacophony of laughter and voices. The smell of burning candles mixed with the heady scent of good ale filled the air as he made his between the men and women sitting at tables.

The flicking candlelight reflected off the walls of dark timber hewn from sturdy English Oak. A long, wooden bar stood along one entire wall with people seated at it, talking and laughing and drinking their pints eagerly. Tables of other patrons filled the rest of this large room while two open entranceways led to smaller and more intimate rooms from which drifted more sounds of merry laughter. The steady clink of pints on tables hinted at a similar occupation.

At the end of the great oak bar, Sarah smiled at him as she picked up a platter filled with pints of ale destined for thirsty patrons. She nodded toward the corner of the large room to a table where four men sat in deep conversation.

Gordon nodded acknowledgement and headed straight for them.

The man sitting against the wall looked up as he approached. He sported a thick beard and dark hair cropped short. He had an air about him -- an air of total confidence and determination.

The stout man next to him roared with laughter and slapped his thigh. He raised his glass and drank deeply but began laughing again, which sent some of the amber fluid flying into the air toward two men at the table with their backs to Gordon.

"Come now, Kempe!" One of the men rose quickly as he wiped the ale off his shirt. "You're supposed to drink good ale, not spit it on your friends so they wear it home!"

In that moment, William Shakespeare turned and faced Gordon Smith.

Gordon was struck by the man's eyes.

Shakespeare's eyes sparkled with a deep intensity, filled with both a burning intelligence and a keen sense of humor. And instantly, he felt that somehow this man could look right through him and see into his innermost thoughts.

His lean, handsome face was lit up with laughter. His slender moustache was complemented by a well-trimmed beard that he wore long over his chin and shorter across the rest of his face. His brown hair was long, reaching the top of his collar.

"Well, sir! You've come at a very historic moment." Shakespeare bowed deeply with a grand sweep of his right arm. He gestured toward the jovial perpetrator. "Will Kempe has just attempted a truly dangerous experiment to see if a man can laugh and drink at the same time. And all with near fatal results!"

The three men seated at the table roared with laughter.

"Alas, he lives on. And now, my shirt must bear the stains of his ill-advised exercise." He turned and laughed along with the others. In a flash, he offered Gordon the empty chair next to him.

"But where's our manners, lads? Here's a chair for our unnamed friend, and I dare think we'll hear some weighty matters from him lest his serious expression tells untruths with the same effect as Will Kempe drinks ale this night!"

Gordon sat in the chair and faced the smiling

87

men.

"I am William Shakespeare." He half-rose again and bowed as he gestured to the others. "Here is the leader of our humble troupe, Richard Burbage. Next to him, the grandest comedian on any stage of London today -- Will Kempe!" He turned to the final man, who now became visible.

"Our dark friend from Africa -- Uri Abada."

Gordon felt his heart skip a beat as he remembered Tom's words.

Although Uri remained seated as he nodded to Gordon, he could tell the man was a giant among men. Gordon guessed he was a full head and shoulders taller than the biggest man in the entire pub. Uri's shoulders were massive; his arms rippled with taut muscles even while he was seated in his chair at rest. But what seemed odd was the man's face. It seemed almost too perfect -- too handsome, as if etched from dark stone. Uri's ebony skin glistened in the candlelight, especially off his clean-shaven head.

But Gordon was struck by the eyes -- again, Gordon felt something stirring when Uri's brown eyes fixed their intent gaze on him. Gordon's hearted pounded with fear and excitement -- as with the thrill of the chase.

Gordon felt an overpowering conviction that he'd met Uri before.

But where?

Shakespeare spread his arms around the table. "And pray, what is your name, good friend?"

"Gordon Smith, sir."

"A noble name, sir. A name common in its

familiarity, and yet uncommon in its personality!" Kempe laughed.

Gordon noticed a momentary smile on Uri's face and then he turned quickly to join Kempe's laughter.

"I must write a play for our new actor." Shakespeare rubbed the beard on his chin in contemplation as he peered at Uri. "He must be a soldier -- no, a warrior prince! A leader of men."

"He must have a pretty wife!" Burbage added.

"Yes! But, not a historical setting this time." Shakespeare drank deeply from his ale as he eyed Uri carefully. "The obvious tale for him would be Hannibal and Rome, but it doesn't seem right ... "

"Not another history play!" Kempe shouted. "We need comedy! We need Falstaff! We need to laugh more, and so do our patrons!"

Shakespeare shook his head firmly. "Perhaps you're right. I have Rome too much on my mind these days -- the noble but tragic figure of Brutus and the murder of Julius Caesar consume my every waking moment lately."

Gordon noticed Sarah serving a table near them. He raised his hand, and she nodded. He held up five fingers, and she nodded and quickly went to the bar.

"A tragedy! Yes, a tragedy with a black man playing the lead!" Shakespeare pounded the table with his fist.

"I don't know where you'll get that story, Will." Burbage snorted. "I've never seen such a play nor read any tragic tale with a black man as the lead. Perhaps a story where he plays one of the leads? But not the lead."

"Then, I'll have to write one myself!"

"Oh my, what have we here? Could it be another sweet Juliet?" Kempe sat up eagerly as Sarah appeared carrying a platter with five pints of ale.

"This round is on me, gentlemen. For the pleasure of your good company this evening," Gordon said.

"I knew I would like this fellow the moment I set eyes on him." Burbage nodded as he took one of the pints.

Uri and Shakespeare each took a pint. Sarah walked around the table and offered the platter to Kempe.

In a flash, Kempe wrapped his arms around Sarah and pulled her onto his lap.

Sarah squealed in surprise and then sat there with a stern expression on her face.

Gordon realized Sarah was about to explode.

"Now, now, Kempe. That's no way to treat a lady," Shakespeare said in a serious tone. "And I believe she is not one with which to trifle."

"She's a barmaid, Will! She's no lady! And I'll trifle with whom I will!" Kemp laughed.

Sarah sat the platter down on the table, picked up two pints of ale and twisted to face Kempe.

"Ah, you are my kind of girl -- going to give me two pints at one time, eh!" Kempe laughed even louder.

"You got that right," Sarah said in a surprisingly calm tone.

And in a single movement, she raised both pints over Kempe's head and poured the amber liquid over his head in a flood of ale.

Everyone within sight of their table shouted out

in laughter as they pointed and stamped their feet.

Kempe gasped for breath and soon released his grasp on Sarah's waist. He wiped the ale out of his nose and beard and laughed jovially at her as she rose.

Sarah stood up calmly and placed the two empty glasses on the platter. She ignored Kempe's non-stop laughter and walked around between Gordon and Shakespeare.

"Now then, will there be anything else, gentlemen?" Sarah looked at each man in turn around the table -- everyone except Kempe.

"Two more pints, miss." Gordon pulled out his money and placed it in Sarah's open hand. "And, we'll be drinking these two, if you don't mind."

She smiled triumphantly at him.

"I told you, Kempe. You must learn to read people, else you'll find yourself in real trouble one day." Shakespeare tipped his glass at Kempe.

"Aye, you're the playwright. I'm just the comic relief."

The conversation meandered from subject to subject for quite some time. Gordon listened carefully and soon discerned the close-knit relationships between Burbage, Kempe and Shakespeare. And yet, although there was a deep respect for each man and his unique talents between the three, there was also an intense rivalry as well -- especially between Kempe and Shakespeare.

But Uri was new to the group -- that alone was obvious. And, he was a man of few words. Gordon couldn't get a read on him at all. And Gordon had an odd feeling as he observed him -- something didn't add up.

"Now then, a new year is almost upon us, and we still have no theater. How can we put on plays when we have no stage? And with no stage, we have no audience. And with no audience, we have no money. And with no money, we must surely die," Shakespeare said with a sad finality.

"A sad state indeed," Burbage agreed.

"Perhaps it's time you moved to another city -- a new audience?" Uri said, a little too eagerly.

"Not so, fellow!" Shakespeare shouted. "London is the heart of England. It is here where we must play -- or we must not play at all."

"Aye, Uri may be right," Will Kempe said with a surprisingly serious tone. "The atmosphere has changed here. Many people are against actors and plays. That's why we can't renew our lease -- the landowner has caved in to the pressure of the community leaders."

"And there have been evil deeds of late," Burbage added with an air of suspense.

"What do you mean?" Gordon asked.

"Two nights ago, as he walked home in the wee hours, Sam Golden was assaulted and left for dead in a dark alley." Burbage shook his head somberly.

"A good actor for the Admiral's Men," Will Kempe added. "He wouldn't hurt a fly. He always plays the female leads."

"And the week before, Arthur Brumbley was brutally attacked and remained unconscious three whole days after they got him to shelter." Burbage held up three fingers for emphasis. "They didn't expect him to live that first night. But, he's a strong one. He pulled through all right."

"Still, someone tried to kill both of them! Neither had money on them, so it wasn't robbery!" Kempe said savagely. "I tell you, they're turning the people against us. I've heard whispers that say all actors -- and playwrights -- are a pariah on good society!"

"Come now, gentlemen," Shakespeare said in a comforting tone. "The authorities are investigating both assaults. We mustn't jump to conclusions. None of these acts may be related. And our problem renegotiating the lease on the Theater is our business matter."

"No, it's not," Burbage argued. "And you know it's not. The owners are cowered by public opinion against us -- against all acting companies in London. We've got to move."

"Let's move south of the Thames, which will put us out of their jurisdiction. And, we'll be right next to London and our audience! We've picked the spot -- now we just need timber to build it." Shakespeare urged with a confident tone.

"Gentlemen, I can't stop thinking about the attacks. There was one thing both assaults had in common." Kempe's voice grew low and mysterious. "Aye, each man was beaten severely. But, I heard that each of them also had these strange claw marks on their arms and on their chests -- almost like some kind of animal had attacked them instead of a man. And though neither got a look at their attacker, each man said he was covered in black cloak and hood."

Gordon took a deep breath and held it.

"All they could see under the black hood were

two glowing red eyes."

Gordon breathed normally again. But now he knew the attacker was Dragnorr or one of his minions.

A tense silence filled the air around the men.

"No, my friends. It is time you moved on. And I'll tell you why." Uri paused as he sipped his ale. "This public opinion didn't come about on its own. No, it was perpetrated from the highest levels of government." Uri smiled as he noted the somber effect of his words.

"The government's afraid of the growing influence of actors and playwrights. Yes, our art can sway public opinion as greatly as any newspaper or political orator. And we don't want to cross swords with them. Remember what happened to Marlowe!"

Shakespeare, Burbage and Kempe all shifted nervously in their chairs at the mention of the great playwright's name.

"That was different. Marlowe got himself involved in spying for the government and then double-crossed the very ones that hired him. He was a young fool. He brought it on himself." Burbage drank deeply of his ale as he glowered at the others.

"But, remember how easy it was for Marlowe to be led to that little room and meet his untimely end. And the men that killed him? All of them got away scot-free." Uri snapped his fingers. "That's because the government was behind it. You can't fight them and hope to win."

"Maybe we should leave London." Shakespeare looked around the table. "Maybe, it's time to cut our losses and move on." The playwright looked from one person to the other a moment and then added, "Maybe it's time I returned to Stratford and gave all this up."

Chapter Ten

Gordon watched Uri closely the rest of the evening. Young Tom Walker was right: something about the dark man didn't add up. And he still had the gnawing feeling that he had met him before -- somehow.

But mostly, he picked up on Uri's subtle messages as he continued to do his best to convince Shakespeare and all 'The Chamberlain's Men' to pick up and leave London.

He strongly suspected Uri was in league with Dragnorr. At the very least, he wasn't who he seemed to be. Either way, he couldn't be trusted.

And just after midnight, when Uri bid them all good night and walked away, Gordon noticed Uri's strange gait. It was almost as if walking on two legs was something new to him.

After they finished their pints a short time later, Kempe and Burbage left for their homes as well.

Gordon Smith and William Shakespeare sat alone at the farthest table in the 'Three-legged Dog.'

Sarah Nightingale walked up and sat down in an empty chair with them.

"We haven't been properly introduced," Shakespeare said with a warm smile. "My name is William Shakespeare, and this is my friend Gordon Smith."

Sarah nodded, smiling. "Miss Sarah Nightingale."

"I must apologize for the behavior of Kempe, Miss Nightingale. A lady must never be treated in such a fashion." Shakespeare lifted his glass towards her.

"You, sir, are a gentleman, even if your friend is a rogue." Sarah laughed. "There was no harm done. It comes with the job."

"But, you are a lady and deserve to be treated as such," Shakespeare said with emotion.

"I am but a humble barmaid, kind sir."

"Does it matter whether a woman is a barmaid or a lady-in-waiting at court? You are both women. Yes, your circumstances differ, but inside your heart, inside your mind ... you are very much the same. It is not our station in life or the clothes we wear that make us people. It is what we are inside our hearts and our minds that make us who we really are. A woman, whether a barmaid or a lady-in waiting, has the same essential wants and needs, the same fears and yearnings, and ultimately treasures the same hopes in life -- love, family, contentment and happiness. And sadly, each will experience very nearly the same tragedies if they walk this earth long enough."

"You speak truth," Gordon agreed in a thoughtful tone.

"Life is truth. Love is truth. But, will another's heart always be true?" Shakespeare sighed with emotion. "Where was I? Oh yes -- that we are alike."

William Shakespeare smiled, and the candlelight glistened off his face.

"Every person who has ever walked this tawdry ground has yearned for happiness and peace, both for himself and for those he loves. And to seek and capture that fleeting and all too elusive spirit we call joy and wrap its glowing tendrils around our hearts and never let it go." Shakespeare spread his arms wide. "We *need* to eat and sleep and work in order to survive ... But even more, we need *love* and *happiness* and *joy* in order to live."

Shakespeare paused a moment as he stroked the beard on his chin.

"And most important of all -- we each need hope. Hope keeps us looking forward. Hope keeps us looking beyond the seemingly unending problems we face each day." Shakespeare nodded silently before he continued.

"If a person loses hope for the future ... he will drown inside the trials of today."

"You understand people quite well," Sarah said with a smile.

"We are all so much alike deep inside ... and yet, we walk this earth alone -- isolated within our minds by our thoughts and our desires and our pain ... *and believe it is only we who feel this way*."

Gordon and Sarah stared in awe.

"I perceive that no matter whether a man is a king or a pauper, a knight or a farmer -- deep inside ... we are all lovers, we are all heroes, we are all stricken by our failings ... and we are all haunted by our fears. If we could but peer inside the hearts of others, we would see ourselves. But, so few *really* look."

"You are a keen observer, my friend." Gordon nodded approval.

"I love people." Shakespeare nodded with a quiet sincerity and an air of sadness.

"I see that love in the speeches by your

characters -- in their passions and in their exploits. You must continue writing plays, good sir. Tell us these great truths about ourselves with your plays." Gordon watched Shakespeare carefully for his reaction.

"Alas, it seems not to be."

"Your plan is good. Build south of the Thames. You will be outside the city's direct jurisdiction, but close enough for your audience." Gordon smiled.

"But these attacks on my fellow actors are ... disturbing."

Gordon and Sarah exchanged glances.

"I've heard about them," Sarah said. "Two of the girls were talking about them earlier. I'm sure the perpetrator will be caught soon. It will end."

"But, if the government is against us, there will be more attacks." Shakespeare shook his head.

"You just played before the queen at court. The entire court enjoyed your latest play?" Gordon nodded.

"Yes, as always, the queen loves a rousing play."

"More likely, these things are instigated by a few people in positions of power, and they do their best to sway others to their thinking. These things rise like a wave and then fade away just as quickly. After all, those who attend your plays are quite enthusiastic in their support, right?" Gordon finished his pint with a long swig.

"Yes, indeed. And *that* is what keeps me going -- when the groundlings shout for lovers to make up and love, when they scream for the death of the enemy who has caused so much pain, when they

99

applaud heartfelt words spoken strong and true --
those very words to which I gave life ... "
Shakespeare paused with a faraway look in his eyes.
"I give the audience love and war and tragedy and
history -- but the story is merely the vehicle ... it is
the people inside the play -- their lives, their loves
and their pain -- with which the audience connect.
My characters speak the words born in my heart and
mind -- words that are mine and now are theirs too.
I see the audience feel them as surely as I felt them
when I wrote them upon paper. It makes us one ... "

"An actor needs an audience," Sarah added.

"A playwright needs an audience even more.
Which is why it saddens me so to even contemplate
leaving my craft and heading home to Stratford. I
feel I have so much more to write!" Shakespeare
downed the remains of his pint in an urgent gulp.

"We'll help you," Gordon said.

"You? How?"

"We're here on ... *official business*, to solve this
crime and see that all actors and playwrights are
safe to carry on their craft in London." Sarah smiled
proudly.

"Yes, I think it's safe to share that with him
now," Gordon added. "Of course, you mustn't tell
the others. It might hamper our, um, investigation."

William Shakespeare looked from Sarah to
Gordon with wide eyes.

"You mean, you're under orders from the
queen?"

"Oh, higher than that," Gordon said with
feeling.

Shakespeare's mouth fell open.

"Well, actually, you're right. We're under orders from the highest authorities." Sarah's eyes burned with disapproval at Gordon.

"My mistake, yes. Sometimes it seems certain circles feel they're more powerful than the queen, you know." Gordon waved his hand nonchalantly.

"Can you protect me?"

"Yes, in fact, you'll be under careful surveillance. We have a good boy, er, man, on the job right now."

"Then, perhaps if this attacker is caught and we have the support of certain individuals in the *highest circles* of government -- perhaps our plans may continue?" Shakespeare's tone grew more hopeful with each word.

"Indeed sir, that is our goal." Sarah smiled broadly.

Shakespeare rose, albeit a bit unsteadily.

"Well then, I'll just go to the privy and give back this ale I so recently borrowed. And yet, I shall walk home a happier man than I arrived."

William Shakespeare stumbled with his first step, knocked over a chair and then promptly fell across Sarah's legs.

"Apologies again, Miss Sarah. I should have tried to stand a bit more carefully, since I seem to have forgotten how much ale I've consumed this enjoyable evening."

After he walked away with unsteady steps, Sarah jumped into the chair next to Gordon.

"I've heard about those two attacks -- and the terrible *thing* that walks the streets of London at night!" she said, out of breath.

"I heard it too. It wears a black cloak and a black hood and peers with glowing red eyes. It must be Dragnorr -- it couldn't be the Anon." Gordon licked his lips.

Sarah nodded quickly. "There's more. The girls told me that there is more than one cloaked figures that walks the streets at night -- and some have no faces! So, the Anon are with him. And, they talk of large, fearsome bats that fly the skies."

"Things are further along than we feared."

"Yes, our enemies are gathered around us and have already put their plan into motion," Sarah said emphatically.

"Sounds like there is a strong company of Shadows and Anon teamed with Dragnorr here."

"Can we let young Tom Walker follow Shakespeare alone? It might be dangerous!" Sarah whispered urgently.

"You're right. And we don't have time to get to our Time Transporters and report to Hylrada either." Gordon thought quickly.

"We've got to hurry; he'll leave the privy any moment." Sarah glanced toward the end of the pub.

"Okay, we'll leave ahead of Shakespeare. We know the way to his house since we parked our Transporters in the alley just down from it. We'll get ahead of him and then keep him in sight behind us."

"Do you think they will attack Shakespeare tonight?" Sarah asked.

"I do. And more, I think the black man who sat at the table with us tonight -- Uri -- I believe he is in league with them somehow. He seemed to recognize my name."

Sarah's eyes widened.

"If I'm right, Uri may be reporting to Dragnorr even as we speak. Yes, I think an attack is imminent."

"I'll grab my coat." Sarah jumped out of her seat. She returned a minute later ready to leave.

Gordon and Sarah walked out the door. Gordon glanced over his shoulder and saw Shakespeare just coming out of the privy.

"We've got to run a few blocks and get a good lead," Gordon whispered.

Sarah took off running with Gordon right behind.

They ran two blocks and then slowed to a walk-run, both fairly out of breath. They walked three more blocks at this quick pace. Finally, they paused and turned around.

Farther down the dark and empty street, they could see the outline of the familiar figure of Shakespeare as he walked a bit unsteadily toward them.

And they noticed the first tendrils of fog slipping from the sky and swirling around them.

Gordon listened intently a moment.

Somewhere in the foggy darkness above, he heard the haunting sound of wings ...

Chapter Eleven

Gordon looked up and down the street. At first, he wasn't quite sure why. It was more like instinct -- and then it hit him. He was looking for a likely spot for an ambush by these creatures of the night.

One block further up, there was gap in the rows of gas lamps that lined the street. The fog was getting thicker, and the darkness would be complete without the glow of a street light right in that spot.

"Sarah, just ahead there -- see?" He pointed out the darkened block.

"Yes, a good place for an ambush," she agreed.

Gordon pulled out his earpiece and inserted it as Sarah did the same. He reached inside his coat pocket and pulled out a stun gun. It was the only real weapon in the stash of technology they found inside their Time Transporters -- and it would only stun its victims unconscious. Sarah pulled hers out of her handbag as well.

"What about the kid?" Sarah whispered. "We can't let him walk into an ambush."

"Right." Gordon considered this aspect a moment. "Okay, I want you to duck inside that small alley right before the darkened section of street. I'll head farther down."

Sarah nodded.

"They won't attack Shakespeare until he's surrounded by the darkness. Tom should show up a bit behind. Get his attention and have him duck into the alley with you."

"What then?" Sarah's eyes grew intent.

"Play it by ear, Sarah. I'm sure you'll know what

to do."

Sarah pulled out her scanner and started to switch it on.

"Hang on. Wait until you hear them attack before you use it. They'll probably have their scanners on and will pick up its signal if you have it on."

"We wait blindly for their attack?"

"We have the element of surprise right now," Gordon reassured her.

Shakespeare's muffled footsteps came to their ears.

Gordon nodded, and Sarah took off for the side alley.

Gordon ran off at a trot. He continued until he was right in the middle of the darkened block.

Gordon eased himself into the deep darkness of a doorway, pressed himself against the hard timber of the door and waited.

He didn't have to wait long.

The fog grew thicker by the second until it was difficult to see even a few feet away. In the distance, the glow of the gas street lanterns farther up the street disappeared inside the fog one by one until only the nearest two were visible.

The darkness was almost complete.

Gordon cringed as the sound of large winged creatures fluttering in the darkness above increased.

"Sarah," Gordon whispered.

"Yes."

"Shadows are all about -- right above me."

"Be careful," she whispered urgently.

"Let me know when you have Tom."

"Yes."

The sound of footsteps grew discernable.

Gordon felt the adrenaline pumping throughout his body as he readied himself.

Shakespeare suddenly appeared out of the darkness and strolled right past him.

Gordon gripped his stun gun tighter.

Shakespeare disappeared into the darkness as suddenly as he appeared. The sound of his receding footsteps grew fainter with each passing second.

Now, an ominous scratching sound came out of the darkness directly above him.

Gordon slowly leaned forward until he could see upward along the edge of the three-story building.

Far above, near the top of the building, a cloaked figure scrambled in a surreal fashion along the face of the bricks. In the darkness, Gordon saw shiny black appendages grabbing hold of the bricks as it scurried along in a terrifying fashion.

The nightmare image came into focus above him; shiny talons on the end of each long, black appendage ripped into the bricks as it clawed its way forward. But a hood covered the strange beast's head and a cloak hid its body from view, preventing Gordon from seeing it completely. One thing was certain: the bizarre creature must be very powerful to scamper so easily across the face of the buildings.

Gordon felt his heart leap into his throat.

"I've got Tom," Sarah's voice whispered in his earpiece.

As he watched in terror, the cloaked figure leaped into the air toward the spot where Shakespeare had just disappeared.

106

A terrified scream pierced the foggy darkness -- and stopped too suddenly.

Gordon burst out of his hiding spot and ran toward the sound.

As he ran, he enabled the scanner in his left hand while he held his stun gun in his right. He glanced at the screen.

Movement was everywhere -- just ahead and above.

The shrieks of Shadows filled the night and sent a chill through his heart.

"They've seen me!" Gordon whispered urgently.

From the darkness overhead, he saw five Shadows diving on him.

His stun gun was set on wide dispersal -- he'd anticipated they would attack first.

He fired three shots.

Three Shadows folded their wings and fell to the snow-covered street while the other two flew off with wild shrieks.

But more attacked.

Gordon fired again and again.

He realized that even though the creatures fell stunned with direct hits, they immediately began fluttering their wings and would quickly recover.

Without warning, two Shadows appeared out of the fog right beside him.

He felt them rip their tiny talons deep into the shoulders of his coat as they beat their large wings against his head. Their talons latched onto him, and they threw their weight against him, attempting to pin him to the ground.

Gordon fell to the ground and quickly rolled

over, lashing out with his arms to loosen their deadly grasp.

Their nightmare shrieks filled the air from every direction now.

Gordon shot again and again in rapid fire.

And suddenly, they were gone.

He panted, out of breath, as he looked all around. But the Shadows were gone; even the ones he had stunned had fled back into the darkness and fog of the sky.

Now, the sound of struggling came to his ears from just beyond his vision.

"Help me!" Shakespeare cried out.

Gordon jumped up.

He glanced at his scanner and saw two figures fighting on the ground right in the middle of the street directly ahead.

As he approached, the struggling stopped, but Shakespeare's muffled cries grew audible. Gordon realized the attacker had him by the throat.

He pocketed his scanner and adjusted his stunner for tight dispersal. He knew this creature ahead was twice the size of a man and four times the size of a Shadow.

Two shadowy figures lying on the ground became visible before him.

Gordon stopped and aimed.

"We meet once again, Gordon Smith."

The hissing voice was incredibly loud and reverberated in the night air.

Gordon stood frozen a moment in shock at hearing the fantastic voice.

In the next instant, he recognized it as the voice

of Dragnorr.

"I thought I'd killed you the last time. And yet, somehow you and your precious Sarah still live!" Dragnorr hissed angrily.

Gordon paused in thought, wishing he could recall that last encounter with Dragnorr -- even the smallest detail. But, he couldn't even remember what Dragnorr looked like -- and the hood still kept his features hidden.

And yet, as he peered, two glowing red eyes became eerily discernable.

"Speak, Gordon! It's not like you to be so quiet!"

"Uh, well ... "

"Have you lost your courage, puny human? Do you fear me at last?"

Gordon held his stunner up to eye level and aimed.

"I'll rip Shakespeare to shreds with my talons if you fire."

"That would be a huge change in the timeline, Dragnorr. Can you risk such a change?" Gordon said at last. He realized if he kept Dragnorr talking, perhaps he might find an opening.

"There is no risk for me. I am not of this world!" he roared.

"Right, then." Gordon moved to the right to try and get a better aim.

Dragnorr shifted his lithe body around while he kept two arms around Shakespeare's neck.

In that moment, Gordon realized that Dragnorr had four legs, each tipped with a single, curved talon. And his legs and arms had no skin -- only a

109

black, bone-like structure.

"So, where is your precious Sarah, Gordon? You two rarely travel alone." Dragnorr's hooded head glanced around.

"I sent her away," Gordon said, though his tone was unsure.

"I must congratulate you on one thing. My Anon have chased you through time, and yet you escape time and time again!"

"We're getting quite good at that actually," Gordon replied confidently. He felt a renewed sense of courage at Dragnorr's words.

"I would like you to explain one thing to me though." Dragnorr's growling returned to a snake-like hiss.

"Go ahead." Gordon continued to edge around, looking for a good shot.

"How are you and Sarah still here?" Dragnorr's hissing faded as the creature paused.

"Well, we're still here, you see … hmmm."

"You shouldn't be here! It's not possible! I calculated my plan most carefully!" Dragnorr's hissing changed into a growling roar.

Gordon's eyebrows rose with intrigue. It sounded like Dragnorr thought he had killed them -- and yet, he didn't say it plainly. His choice of words was ... odd.

"Perhaps I could ask you a question and that would help both of us?" Gordon asked.

"Speak, Gordon Smith. I tire of this game! I have Shakespeare in my talons, and the night won't last forever!"

"What exactly ... " Gordon paused. He didn't

want Dragnorr to realize that he couldn't remember anything from their previous encounter. It probably wouldn't be a good idea.

"Speak, Gordon!"

"I mean ... it's just a little fuzzy, you know -- our last encounter. Not all of it, just bits and pieces, you see. If you'd tell me just a little more detail on how you *tried* to kill us last time, well then, I'll tell you how we escaped."

"*What?*"

Dragnorr released one of his talons around Shakespeare's throat and rose to face Gordon more directly.

Gordon cringed as the glowing red eyes within the hood blazed at him.

"Escape! You think you escaped from me?"

"Hmmm, maybe that's not the right word," Gordon ran his hands through his brown hair, realizing he might have made a mistake.

"You don't remember, do you?" Dragnorr hissed loudly.

"Oh no, that's not it at all. I can remember -- sort of. No, no." Gordon stepped back as his mind raced.

"Yessssss!" Dragnorr hissed confidently. "I anticipated that you and Sarah would simply ... *disappear* when I went back to destroy ... But no! Now it begins to make sense." He pointed a shiny black talon at Gordon.

"No, no, there's nothing here that's making any sense," Gordon said with shrinking confidence. "Don't fool yourself on that one! I'm positive nothing's making any sense!"

Dragnorr loosened his last talon from around

111

Shakespeare as he raised himself higher to face Gordon.

"That's why you didn't flee back to Hylrada right away! That's why it was so difficult to find you. You didn't return to your usual spots. No, my Anon found you in all those odd times -- your Transporters still in disrepair. And *that's* why you didn't -- " Dragnorr froze in mid-sentence.

Gordon felt his spirit sinking as rapidly as Dragnorr stood up.

Suddenly, Shakespeare knocked Dragnorr's grip loose and in one quick movement rolled out from underneath him.

"*What?*" Dragnorr roared as he looked around rapidly.

Gordon felt his courage return. He fired his stunner right at Dragnorr's head.

Dragnorr roared in pain. He fell right on his back -- and right back on top of Shakespeare.

"Oh no! That's not good!" Gordon shouted.

"Help!" Shakespeare yelled.

Dragnorr's six talon-tipped appendages lashed out in every direction as he moaned and growled in a confused daze.

Gordon fired again -- but nothing happened.

He checked his stunner and realized it was out. He reached in his pocket for a fresh charge.

Out of the foggy darkness two Anon appeared, their featureless silver faces screaming rage and anger.

Gordon sent his fist into the first one's midsection, causing him to bow over in pain. But the other leaped on him, sending him to the ground.

Gordon struggled with him, rolling along the ground and exchanging punches. In the background, he heard Dragnorr groaning as he began to come around.

Suddenly, he heard a stunner firing. In the next instant, the Anon he was fighting fell limp.

"I got him, Gordon!" Sarah shouted triumphantly.

"Look out!" Tom Walker yelled fearfully.

Shadows attacked from out of the sky through the fog -- dozens dove upon them from every direction.

The air shook with their wild, haunting shrieks.

Gordon and Tom flailed away with their fists at the creatures trying to latch onto them and pull them down.

Sarah fired her Stunner again and again.

It seemed that everywhere he turned, Shadows shrieked and attacked while Tom yelled and Sarah fired volley after volley.

And as suddenly as the attack started -- it was over.

Gordon jumped up with surprise. He turned all around, but the only evidence of their battle was the badly trampled snow.

"The fallen Shadows must have taken their stunned fellows with them!" Gordon shouted.

"Where'd they go?" Sarah asked with surprise. She turned rapidly around, pointing her stunner.

"What were they?" Tom asked breathlessly.

"They seemed some sort of gargoyles?" Shakespeare stood beside Sarah, panting from his exertions.

"Well ... no, not quite." Gordon's expression changed from a deep frown furrowed in thought into one of half-questioning concern edged with humor.

"More like flying monkeys." Gordon laughed mischievously. "Frightening and scary flying monkeys, yes. But, not flying gargoyles."

"*What?*" Shakespeare shouted in disbelief.

"Perhaps flying baboons?" Sarah suggested

Gordon smiled at her.

"Could be, Sarah. Or ... flying chimpanzees? Yes, they're quite fierce, you know, but Shadows are about one quarter their size with no fur."

"Right! In fact, their skin absorbs light -- that's why they are darker than the darkness and why it's so hard to see them." Sarah's eyes twinkled as she got into the spirit.

"Indeed, all you can really see is movement -- can't quite make them out at all really," Gordon added.

"But you can hear their wings when they're coming for you." Sarah shivered at the thought.

"Whatever they were -- they were flying!" Shakespeare shouted with frustration. "They seemed a nightmare come alive! And the creature that had me by the throat -- his eyes glowed red as burning coals!"

"Dragnorr! We let him escape! We had him ... Oh no!" Gordon hit himself in the forehead with the palm of his hand. "It must have been a diversion -- that last attack. We were so busy fighting the Shadows off that ... " Gordon paused.

"Dragnorr and his Anon escaped," Sarah

finished for him.

Gordon bent over and examined the ground. He began walking in wider and wider circles searching vainly for signs of Dragnorr and his minions – and then searching the dark shadows, searching the corners of buildings and looking down all the nearest alleys.

But they were all gone.

Chapter Twelve

Gordon and Sarah escorted Shakespeare to the door of his house. They sent Tom home right after telling him to be at the 'Three-legged Dog' the next evening to receive further direction.

Finally alone, Sarah and Gordon walked a block south until they came to a little alley.

Gordon pulled the key out from around his neck and held it up to air.

A door appeared, and they both walked inside.

"We better report to Hylrada." Sarah sat down on a chair near a bank of consoles.

"Yes, I thought of that already." Gordon walked over to the repaired communication console and activated it.

The furry visage of Hylrada appeared.

"Hello, Gordon. Hello, Sarah." Hylrada smiled contentedly at them from the screen as his six ears wiggled with delight. His expression quickly changed to one of deep concern.

"Oh my, is there something the matter? You two look a bit worse for wear tonight."

"We've had a run in with Dragnorr," Sarah replied.

"And some Anon and a few dozen Shadows thrown in for good measure," Gordon added quickly.

"Are you all right?" Hylrada asked soothingly.

"A few bumps and bruises, but nothing serious," Sarah said in a cheery voice.

"Nothing that will leave a scar, at any rate." Gordon sighed tiredly.

"Good, good." Hylrada looked from one to the other a moment. "And what about our friend, William Shakespeare? Is he all right?"

"A little too much ale tonight. I think he has more bruises from falling than from the Shadow's attack. He'll live to write another play," Gordon said.

"That is the point -- will he write another play?" Hylrada asked.

"Well, Dragnorr has set some events in motion that have definitely discouraged him. And in fact, he's thinking of leaving London entirely and making an early retirement back to Stratford." Gordon peered at Hylrada a moment. "And of course, Dragnorr tried to kill him just now, so it could be that when Shakespeare wakes up in the morning he might just pack his bags and head back to the country. Who knows?"

"We must prevent that," Hylrada said firmly.

"Oh, Gordon!" Sarah said with exaggerated exasperation. "Don't paint it so bleak!"

"Well, Sarah and I did have a talk with him. We encouraged him to stick it out -- keep his chin up and all that -- and we reassured him that the whole world wasn't out to get him. In fact, a good majority of London admires him and wants more plays, in spite of the vocal disapproval of a few in power within the city's bureaucracy."

"And did he listen?" Hylrada asked.

Gordon nodded enthusiastically and glanced at Sarah.

"Yes, I think we encouraged him. He seemed a bit more determined to carry on," Sarah agreed.

"Good, good! Now, if we can get Dragnorr and his minions out of London -- out of this time period altogether -- perhaps Shakespeare and history will stay its course."

Gordon and Sarah exchanged glances.

"And how are we to do that on our own?" Sarah asked.

"I'll report to the, um, well ... I'll tell the Temporal Authorities! Yes, that's it! I'll tell them you have indeed made contact with Dragnorr and request reinforcements."

"Okay ... " Gordon said, somewhat unconvinced. "And when will they arrive?"

"Well, these things take time, you know. Procedures must be followed, the proper reports filed."

"How long?" Gordon asked firmly.

Hylrada shifted in his seat nervously and looked off in the distance.

"A day, maybe less."

"So, I guess we've got to keep Dragnorr away from Shakespeare in the meantime?" Gordon shifted in his seat.

"Absolutely. Great idea. And, I'll work on getting you some ... help."

"There is something else." Sarah stood up and walked up to the screen. "Dragnorr said some strange things to us. He said he was surprised we were still here."

"Yes, he said he had expected we would simply -- *disappear*." Gordon added.

"Disappear?" Hylrada rubbed his chin in thought.

"He started to say something else ... now, what was it." Gordon closed his eyes in concentration, trying to remember the exact words. He snapped his fingers.

"I got it. He said -- or started to say -- that he 'went back to destroy ... '"

"Went back!" Hylrada shook his head with a pained expression.

"What does that mean?" Sarah asked.

"Went back -- in time," Gordon suggested.

"I'm afraid it fits the facts," Hylrada said with a hint of sadness.

"Facts?" Gordon and Sarah said together.

"You two had better sit down first."

Gordon and Sarah looked at each other with puzzled expressions. They both sat down and faced the screen.

"For the last few years, ever since you went missing, I have searched for Gordon Smith and Sarah Nightingale throughout Earth's timeline. I have searched through every century and every decade of Earth's history. I've searched records, databases, microfilm and even newspapers. I even searched through all of your pre-technology centuries, searching for even the slightest clues, all in the off chance I could find a hint of the original age in which you existed." Hylrada sighed with a distinct sadness.

"And ... " Gordon and Sarah said together.

"*I couldn't find you.*"

"What does that mean?" Gordon asked quizzically. "We have to be somewhere."

Hylrada moved in his seat uncomfortably. His

119

green eyes glanced around at everything except Gordon and Sarah. Finally, he spoke in a subdued voice.

"Neither you nor Sarah exist in the normal space-time continuum of Earth."

"We don't exist ...?" Sarah repeated in confusion.

"Of course, we exist. I'm sitting here right before you. And, you're sitting right there. You feel pretty real to me." Gordon patted her arm.

Sarah jerked her arm away as her expression turned to panic.

"We don't exist. Don't you get it? Think about what Hylrada just said!" Sarah yelled.

"But, that can't be right. Can it, Hylrada?" Gordon turned to the alien on the screen.

"You don't exist -- at least not in the space-time continuum. You have no history, you have no past -- you don't exist," he said simply.

"But, we're here!" Gordon protested.

"I realize that. And, I've got some theories." Hylrada smiled half-heartedly.

"Theories!" Sarah yelled angrily.

"Well, yes. One must theorize when there are so few facts."

"I don't want theories; I want to know who I am!" Sarah stood and pointed at Hylrada. "I want to know who my parents were and where I was born and ... and ... " Sarah put her hand to her face and turned away.

"We don't exist?" Gordon repeated.

"Not in the normal space-time continuum." Hylrada placed his hands together patiently and looked from one to the other.

Gordon felt a sudden dizziness. The universe around him spun out of control a moment. He waited a bit until the vortex cleared somewhat before he asked the obvious question.

"Is that bad?"

Sarah jumped up and punched Gordon on the arm as hard as she could.

"Ow! That hurt!"

"I meant it to!"

Gordon rubbed his arm painfully. "I don't get it. If I don't exist, why does my arm hurt?"

"You both exist, but you exist solely in the ether between time and space."

Two tears rolled slowly down Sarah's cheeks. Gordon's mouth dropped open in shock.

"But, we're human, aren't w-we?" Sarah's voice shook with emotion.

"Yes, absolutely."

"We just don't exist, that's all." Gordon smirked.

Sarah punched him again.

"Ow ... "

"Really, I'm very sorry about all this. I tried to find some evidence, any kind, that you were born, you lived, you got married, you paid taxes, you got in trouble with the law -- anything. There is just nothing -- nothing that references either a Gordon Smith or a Sarah Nightingale in any part of Earth's timeline." Hylrada sighed.

"We don't exist ... " Sarah said sadly.

"For someone who doesn't exist, I sure am depressed." Gordon shook his head with a pained expression.

Sarah breathed deeply and put her hands on her hips. "I'm leaving."

She walked toward the door, which opened with a flash of light.

"Where are you going?" Gordon asked plaintively.

"To my Time Transporter. I need to think."

"Please, don't go."

"Why?"

"Because then I won't exist and I'll be alone too!"

"Oh, get a life!" Sarah shouted.

"I have to exist before I can get a life."

Sarah turned and stormed out. The door flashed shut automatically.

He turned back to the screen, where Hylrada stared at him with a somber expression. Gordon rubbed his eyes deep in thought before he spoke.

"So, how do you think this happened?"

"What do you mean?" Hylrada asked.

"You know, how come we don't exist anywhere in Earth's history?"

"Oh, I have a few theories."

"I'm kind of tired -- how about just give me your best shot?"

"Okay." Hylrada paused a moment as he searched his notes. "Yes, well, I think the most likely theory is that someone or something has purposely removed you from history or, more succinctly, prevented you both from ever being born -- you never existed. And, I suspect it was Dragnorr. It sounds like something he would contrive in his twisted mind. And, he did hate you and Sarah."

"Ah, so it was premeditated."

"Yes, that would explain the total absence of any evidence -- the absence of even the slightest hint that either of you ever lived."

"Okay, now I'm feeling depressed again." Gordon stared at Hylrada. "Why would Dragnorr go to such lengths to eradicate Sarah and myself like that? I mean, he must have done a lot of planning and gone to a lot of trouble to pull it off."

"That is the real question now. But not why. If we can find out *how* he did it, perhaps ... "

"But, how is it we didn't simply disappear?" Gordon asked emphatically.

"I've got some theories on that too."

"Your best one, please."

"Well, you were both living in the ether, traveling through time, when he pulled it off. If you weren't time travelers -- if you had been living in one of the ages of Earth's space-time history, then when he pulled off the deed you would have simply disappeared. In fact, Dragnorr is the perpetrator of many similar crimes, including purposely changing history for his own evil ends, and individuals have simply disappeared -- erased from history."

"So, we were outside of time at the time."

"Yes, living in the ether outside time. I think that's why you still exist -- sort of."

A tense silence filled the Time Transporter.

"The link is fading. We'd best call it a night." Hylrada said.

"I do have one last question." Gordon stepped closer to the monitor.

"Go ahead."

"Do you think this has something to do with our memory problems, then?"

Chapter Thirteen

Gordon Smith slept late the next morning.

When he finally forced himself out of bed and looked in the mirror, he turned around and went straight back into bed and slept a few more hours.

Sometime after midday he finally got up, showered and shaved, and ate a spot of breakfast.

He walked outside and took two steps to the right and held up his key to the air. The door appeared, and he stepped inside Sarah's Transporter.

But she was gone.

He searched diligently, but there wasn't even a note. He put in his earpiece and called to her.

She didn't answer.

Gordon walked the streets of London alone the rest of that cold December day, 1598. There wasn't much else he could do.

After all, he didn't exist.

As the sun set beyond the western horizon, he made his way to the Three-legged Dog. After all, he had to protect Shakespeare.

And, he sure needed a good pint of ale.

Or two ...

He found Shakespeare sitting between Will Kempe and Richard Burbage -- at the very table he'd found them the night before.

"So, let me ask you something, William," Gordon said as he sat down and joined them.

"Ask away, Gordon. I'll be happy to enlighten you, lad!" Shakespeare raised his pint toward him.

"If you're here at the pub every night, when do you have time to write?"

The table erupted in laughter.

"Well then, you're right. If I was at a pub every night, I'd never get anything done, would I?" Shakespeare leaned back and sipped his ale. "Normally, I write most every day -- sometimes for hours -- sometimes all evening too. When the muse strikes, I write."

Richard slapped Shakespeare on the shoulder. "But, it's been a bad month, eh?"

"More like several," Shakespeare admitted. "I've just not had any inspiration with all that's going on. And if I can't write." He turned to Kempe and Burbage and smiled. "And if we can't act ... "

"We drink!" they said together.

"Good idea," Gordon said.

Gordon noticed that Uri was nowhere to be seen -- which was good. But, he also noted that Sarah was nowhere to be seen. He had expected her to be here working as a barmaid, helping him guard Shakespeare.

Well, there was a job to do whether Sarah took it seriously or not.

He quickly drank his first pint and ordered a second.

The room was filled with laughter, but Gordon didn't really feel like laughing.

After some time, Shakespeare leaned over and put his arm around Gordon's shoulders.

"Gordon, you've barely said a word all evening -- and you've barely cracked a smile, much less laughed along with the rest of us. And Kempe here has kept us in stitches."

Shakespeare's eyes grew concerned.

"Come now; tell us what's troubling you, lad."

Gordon tipped his pint up and drained it. He sat it down firmly on the table and looked William Shakespeare right in the eye.

"I don't exist."

Shakespeare sat back with a shocked expression etched on his face.

Silence filled the table.

And then a roar of laughter drowned out the rest of the pub.

"Gordon, you do exist!" Kempe cried out with a big smile. "You're sitting at the table with us drinking pints!"

Gordon's face grew serious. "But do you know my parents? Do you know where I was born?"

"Gordon, we've just met you. Of course we don't." Richard slammed his drink down and sent some amber liquid flying. "You don't know my parents either, do you? Nor the village I was born. We've just met!"

Gordon sat up straighter and gathered his wits.

"But you do know your parents. And you know where you were born, right?"

Richard's eyes widened with surprise. "Of course I do."

"Well, I don't know my parents or where I was born. In fact, I never had parents and I was never born. Hence, I don't exist. And let me tell you -- it's not a good feeling."

"There's an easy explanation for that one!" Will Kempe's eyes twinkled brightly. "It means you're simply an orphan!"

Gordon grabbed his pint and went to drink but

instantly realized it was empty. He dutifully raised his hand for another.

"Hold, good sir," Shakespeare sat a moment in thought. "I see you sitting there. I see you breathing and drinking."

"And your point?" Gordon asked defensively.

"You must exist, man. Why, we're conversing. I assume you must be thinking in order to form words and express keen ideas." Shakespeare smiled broadly. "Strike that last one, eh."

Kempe slapped Shakespeare across his shoulders as the table erupted again with laughter.

Richard Burbage suddenly stood. He lifted one arm upward and struck a dignified pose. As he gazed far off, his expression became one of quiet tranquility. And right before their eyes, the great actor transformed himself into one of his characters.

Everyone watched carefully -- even those at nearby tables paused in their conversations and waited.

"Do we exist? Are we alive? What is life? What is existence?" Burbage paused dramatically. He turned and reached out to everyone. "Is life merely a dream from which we will awaken and quickly forget this brief but troubled reverie?"

A hush fell on the entire pub.

Will Kempe rose and spread his arms wide as he struck a dramatic and yet overly exaggerated pose. He mimicked Burbage exactly, but his face lit up with humor instead of Burbage's deeply thoughtful demeanor.

"Do we exist? Are we alive? How can we *really* know?" Kempe shouted urgently. He turned to everyone exactly as Burbage had a moment before. "I ask you, good people ... If we drink ale ... will we piss? Of course we will! That is my evidence to prove this is not a dream!"

A roar of laughter greeted his words as Kempe danced a jig and elicited even more laughter.

"I think, therefore -- I am!" shouted an unseen voice above the roar of laughter.

"I *drink*, therefore -- I am!" shouted another in comic response.

The air shook with laughter.

Shakespeare now stood, and another hush fell upon the room. He looked around upon the expectant faces a moment, as if contemplating the deepest recesses of philosophy. His gaze paused on Gordon Smith.

Finally, he spoke. "Do I exist? Or, do I not? That is the ultimate question."

Gordon chuckled. He rose and stood beside William Shakespeare.

"I like it better the way you wrote it."

"What is that?"

Gordon raised one hand toward the ceiling, swayed unsteadily a moment, and spoke. "To be ... or not to be. *That*, is the question."

Shakespeare exchanged puzzled glances with Burbage and Kempe, who shook their heads in return.

"Gordon, I've not written that, though I like it tremendously."

Gordon froze. He stared at Shakespeare a moment.

"Hamlet -- one of his greatest speeches. And

you wrote it," Gordon said in a low voice.

"I'm mulling the idea of writing Hamlet. But I've not quite got around to it just yet."

Gordon sat down quickly.

"Oops."

Chapter Fourteen

She couldn't sleep.

All night long, Sarah Nightingale tossed back and forth in her bed with her troubled thoughts. Sleep eluded her as the words of Hylrada echoed in her mind.

She didn't exist. She had no parents -- she had no past.

Who was she?

As the morning sun rose in the east, she dressed quickly. She carefully put on her makeup and selected her shoes. Sarah took a long time fixing her hair, and in the end put in two blue ribbons.

She looked at herself in the mirror and smiled.

She felt pretty.

But Sarah Nightingale didn't know what to do now. And no matter what thoughts came to her mind, nothing seemed right. Indeed, she felt out of place.

But she felt an overwhelming need to do something!

And so, Sarah did what any self-respecting woman of any century would do ...

She went shopping.

Sarah walked by countless shop windows and peered inside at bundles of lace, rows of hats, and countless shoes of every kind and description.

She shopped and shopped until she was famished. And after eating a bite at a busy pub, she shopped some more.

By mid-afternoon her spirits were much improved.

131

At that point she suddenly realized that Gordon must miss her.

She asked the store to arrange a carriage for her. When it arrived she bundled her boxes of goodies inside and settled herself inside in a little corner of the seat -- the only spot not occupied by one of her purchases.

"Where to, lady?" the driver asked as he shut the door for her.

"Bishopsgate, please. And, hurry!"

He tipped his hat, stepped up top and sat down. He grabbed the reins and shook them hard. The horse took off at a fast trot.

She felt bad now. She had spent most of the day shopping and hadn't said a word to Gordon. He had probably come over to her Transporter and found her missing. He was probably worried about her and wondering where she was.

Sarah expected to find a note or a message inside her Transporter.

She was disappointed when she found neither.

Glancing at the clock, she realized she needed to grab a bite to eat and try to get a little rest before she went off to work the evening at the pub. At least, that was her plan.

She changed into a comfortable dress and sat down for a little supper. Immediately, a heavy tiredness came over her. Her eyes felt so heavy, and her shoulders ached.

Sarah decided to take a quick nap.

And that was her undoing.

Even as her head lay on the pillow, she fell into a deep sleep. The previous night without sleep and her long day shopping all around London had taken its toll.

Sarah fell into the deepest of slumber.

She slept throughout the entire night and awoke early the next morning.

She awoke with a start and immediately sat up in bed. She looked around and recognized her bedroom inside her Transporter. Sarah glanced over at the chronometer.

"Oh no!" she shouted as she jumped onto the floor.

She was still fully dressed except she was barefooted. She grabbed her shoes and ran toward the door. At just that moment, the alarm sounded.

"What is that?" she wondered out loud as she ran over to a console that flickered to life. As she watched, the alley outside grew into focus. She realized the alarm was the one preset to identify Tom Walker and not the others set to trigger when any Shadows or Anon approached their Transporters.

She waited for the right moment. After all, her sudden appearance would be startling enough for the young boy.

As she watched, Tom stopped and began slowly turning as he looked for any sign of her or Gordon. Finally, he turned his back to the Transporter.

She ran outside, engulfed in the momentary burst of light as the door opened.

Tom jumped clean off the ground at the sudden sound of her footsteps directly behind him.

Sarah chuckled when Tom turned around with wide eyes.

"Oh! There you are." He looked around behind her at the empty alley. "What? Where did you come from, then?"

"Never mind that." Sarah walked forward, took Tom by the hand and looked down at him. "What happened last night? Was there any trouble?"

"None of those big bats attacked us, if that's what you mean." Tom smiled.

"Good." Sarah put her hands on her hips. "What about Mr. Smith and Mr. Shakespeare?"

"Oh, they had a good time all right."

Sarah rolled her eyes. "I was afraid of that. Things got a bit out of hand with them?"

"A little." Tom laughed. "They were looking for you all night, especially Mr. Smith. He kept asking for you."

Sarah felt a warm feeling inside her heart -- it was nice to be missed.

"Right, where are they now?"

"Oh, the whole gang went over to Mr. Burbage's flat. A rum sight they all were too." Tom's eyes twinkled with delight.

"What do you mean?"

"The four of them stumbled around the entire way, each trying to keep an eye out for those big bats, and so they kept looking up at the sky and losing their balance. And having a pint or so too many, they kept falling into each other and sometimes flat out on the ground!" Tom laughed out loud. "But oddly, they were singing and laughing the entire time."

"A bit drunk, were they?"

"Some of the worst singing I've heard my entire

life!"

Sarah shook her head disapprovingly. "I'm surprised they made it to Burbage's flat at all."

"I was keeping an eye out for them, my lady! I was never far behind them." Tom thumped his chest proudly.

"Good lad." Sarah put her hand on Tom's shoulder and squeezed appreciatively. She turned toward the street. "Right, then, let's have a visit to Mr. Burbage's flat."

They walked for almost an hour through the streets of London before they reached the address and stood in front of the wooden door. Sarah walked up and pounded hard with the palm of her hand.

She stood back and smiled down at Tom a moment.

The door opened.

Richard Burbage raised his hand over his face and squinted at them.

"Hello? Who's that at this ungodly hour of the morning?"

"It's me, Mr. Burbage. Sarah Nightingale from the pub."

"What?" Burbage swayed unsteadily as he blinked his eyes rapidly trying to adjust to the sunlight. "Oh, I see now. You're the barmaid, right?"

"Yes. Can I come in please? And my young friend too?"

Burbage made a grand, sweeping gesture and invited them both inside.

He led them through a small foyer into a room

off to the right. Sarah stopped in surprise just inside.

On one couch, Will Kempe lay on his back with his arms thrown out to each side. He was still asleep and snored so loudly it seemed he surely must wake himself any moment. He was still fully clothed.

Richard Burbage collapsed back onto the other couch. The pillow and blanket provided evidence he had slept there the night before -- fully clothed as well. He placed his hand over his forehead as if in deep contemplation, though Sarah guessed -- correctly -- he was trying to soothe his aching head.

Gordon Smith lay flat on the floor, snoring as loudly as Will Kempe. In fact, between the two it seemed to Sarah they were both in some contest to see who could snore the loudest.

Sarah walked over to Gordon and kicked his leg.

"Gordon! Wake up!"

"Wha?" Gordon opened his eyes painfully and immediately placed both his hands over his face. "Ohhhhh, my head. Why is the room spinning?"

"Gordon, get up," Sarah ordered in a firm voice.

"Sarah, please. Let me just lie here a moment until the room stops spinning."

Will Kempe sat up. He seemed to go from slumber to being wide awake instantaneously. He stared at her with a puzzled expression.

"Aren't you the barmaid?" he asked.

"Yes, I am." Sarah smiled tepidly at him.

"Good, bring us another round of your best ale, eh? I'm buying this time, lads." Will sat forward and rubbed his hands eagerly.

"Kempe!"

William Shakespeare stood up groggily from

behind the couch. He rubbed his eyes a moment and looked around at each person in the room. He leaned over the back of the couch to steady himself.

"Kempe, we're not at the pub. In fact, the night has passed us by, and we now find ourselves sleeping off the effects of all the pints we previously consumed." Shakespeare rubbed the sides of his head tenderly. "And I for one am quite ready to swear off ale for all time -- for fear my head may soon explode."

"Oh, Shakespeare. Be a man!" Kempe looked back up at Sarah. "We mustn't cast a blind eye on this most fortuitous entrance. I mean, why else would the barmaid come here if not to offer us ale?"

Sarah crossed her arms and tapped her foot impatiently.

"Actually, I've come to protect you."

The four men stopped rubbing their heads, eyes and temples and stared at her.

"Say that again?" Burbage asked with a quizzical expression.

"I've come to protect you."

Gordon stumbled to his feet and swayed unsteadily. He addressed the three men.

"Sarah is right. We must protect you." Gordon swayed too far to one side and suddenly grabbed the arm of a chair so he didn't fall over completely.

"Yes, I feel safer already." Shakespeare chuckled as he slapped Gordon on the shoulder.

Gordon fell to his knees laughing. He stayed a moment in that fashion and with much effort managed to stand again.

"Now, where was I?" Gordon looked at Sarah.

"We're here to protect them," Sarah said as she rolled her eyes.

"Right." Gordon took an unsteady step and almost fell again. "First, we must have a plan."

"Really, I don't know how any of you survived the night without me," Sarah said with exasperation. "How is it Dragnorr didn't kill every last one of you?"

"Dragnorr?" Kempe, Burbage and Shakespeare said together.

"The creature who stalks the streets at night," Sarah said impatiently. "The one with glowing red eyes. He's always accompanied by large, bat-like creatures that shriek and howl."

"Oh, that Dragnorr." Shakespeare nodded.

"What's this?" Burbage asked.

"Those were the creatures we kept a sharp eye out for last night, eh?" Kempe added with a wink and a nod.

"Flying creatures?" Burbage repeated. He stared at Gordon. "I thought you said they were just bats?"

"Really, *really* big bats," Gordon emphasized carefully.

"I thought they were flying monkeys?" Shakespeare rubbed his face. "You said they were more like flying monkeys and not like gargoyles."

"What?" Burbage and Kempe asked together.

"Never mind that." Gordon took a deep breath.

"I thought you were jesting about them," Burbage said with a stern tone. "After all, you filled the evening with your jokes about not existing."

Sarah turned to Gordon.

"You told them that we don't exist!" she shouted

angrily.

"I was a bit depressed. I needed to talk to someone," Gordon pleaded. "And you were nowhere to be found. I mean, where were you?"

"I went shopping."

Gordon's mouth dropped open.

"What were you thinking? I mean, why don't you just go ahead and tell them everything and corrupt the timeline," Sarah said in a stern tone.

"Well, I didn't think telling them about my personal problem would do much harm." Gordon shrugged.

"We got some good laughs out of it too." Kemp chuckled.

Sarah turned and walked toward the door.

"Where are you going?" Gordon asked.

"I'm going to talk with Hylrada. All of you stay here; I'll be back before the sun sets."

"Wait a bit. I'll come too." Gordon took a step forward and fell to the floor, knocking over a chair at the same time.

Sarah paused and glanced back in response to the crashing sound. She shook her head.

"Just wait here with them, Gordon. It will be safer for everyone."

"What about me, mum?" Tom Walker asked eagerly.

"Stay here and keep them out of trouble."

Sarah opened the door and stepped outside. She couldn't afford to walk back, so she watched for a carriage.

Almost at once, a black carriage stopped right in front of her. She felt her heart pounding inside her chest. But, she shook off the feeling of impending danger -- the carriage had appeared so suddenly it had simply startled her. And besides, she needed a ride.

And yet, as she looked up at it, its overall appearance struck fear.

The carriage was completely black in color and was pulled by two black horses. And even more, the windows were all filled with black curtains so that nothing inside was visible.

She looked up at the driver.

And now, fear struck her heart.

The driver sat looking straight forward, dressed completely in black and wearing a black top hat.

The door opened suddenly.

Sarah turned to run.

Two surly-looking men standing on the street next to her grabbed her roughly.

Before Sarah could scream, one covered her face as the other grabbed her around the waist, lifted her up and carried her to the waiting carriage.

Sarah bit the man's hand as hard as she could.

He screamed and drew back his hand.

"Gordon! Help me!" Sarah shouted as the other man threw her inside the dark confines of the black carriage.

The door shut behind her, and the carriage surged forward with the horses at a full gallop at the crack of the driver's whip.

As she lay on the floor, she looked up and saw a dark figure deep inside the shadows, and as her eyes slowly adjusted to the intense darkness, the other's form began to take shape.

140

Sarah gasped.

Two red eyes glowed down upon her from the shadowy outline.

Dragnorr laughed with an evil, hissing tone.

Chapter Fifteen

"They got her!" Tom shouted.

Gordon stumbled outside and immediately was blinded by the morning sun. He shaded his eyes and looked down the street towards the sound of the speeding carriage.

He felt his heart sink at the sight of the black carriage.

Suddenly, one of the black curtains parted and Sarah stuck her head outside.

"Gordon!"

She was immediately pulled back inside by some unseen personage.

"Over there!" Tom pointed the opposite direction.

Gordon groaned as he lost his balance. But, he turned as quickly as he could without falling on his face.

He saw two men racing through the crowds.

Gordon leaned back against the wall as his head spun out of control.

"What are you going to do?" Tom shouted.

"First!" Gordon raised a forefinger. "You've got to stop shouting."

"But, they're all getting away!"

"I know." Gordon took a deep breath and started running toward the carriage. When it turned the corner and disappeared, Gordon stopped and stared.

"You'll never catch it."

"I know."

"How will you rescue her?" Tom pleaded.

Gordon snapped his fingers confidently. "I need

help -- and I know exactly who I need."

"Shall I go with you?"

"No, you stay here as Sarah instructed. I'll go and get hold of Hylrada and tell him the latest turn of events, and I'm going to request some help here."

Gordon arrived inside his Transporter an hour later. He raced inside and hit the switches on the communication console. A few moments later, the familiar six-eared furry face smiled back at him.

"Hello, Gordon."

"We need help! Send in the reinforcements! Send in the Temporal Police ... or whatever you call them. But, send them now!" Gordon shouted.

"Now, now. Tell me what's happened, Gordon."

Gordon quickly recounted the events of the morning.

"So, Dragnorr has Sarah." Hylrada shook his head.

"Are you sure?"

"Pretty much. Black carriage, dark curtains -- only way he can travel in daylight."

"Right! Well, send us the reinforcements, and we'll go rescue her," Gordon said.

Hylrada bit his lip and paused. Finally, he spoke.

"Well, that will be a little difficult."

"Why? Didn't you report to the authority and tell them it's Dragnorr? And he's out to change time and history here!"

"Well, to be completely honest ..." Hylrada shifted in his chair nervously.

"Okay, spill it."

"I am the Temporal Authority."

143

Gordon stared in silence.

"You ... are it."

"Um ... yes."

"I thought you said it was some kind of organization? And there were reinforcements!"

"Well, there is -- sort of. I mean, I do have contacts throughout time. And I do monitor the temporal integrity for problems."

"But ... no police?"

"No. I strictly do monitoring." Hylrada smiled broadly.

"Don't you travel through time and fix things?"

"Oh no, much too dangerous. I told you that before. Traveling through time is tricky -- and filled with dangers."

"You don't travel through time?"

"Once or twice, but not any more. In fact, I gave my only two Time Transporters to you and Sarah back when your original was destroyed by Dragnorr. Nasty encounter, that one."

"Before we lost our memories?"

"Yes."

"So, what do you do when you find a problem? Who do you call? Who do you report to?"

"Well, if it is something bad, I consult with other temporal scientists like myself. I have a number of contacts on various worlds and in various ages."

"And if it's something really bad? Like this!"

"Well, I did have two very good agents who could fix about anything. Both had excellent skills and were very resourceful. We worked together to protect the timeline ... "

144

Gordon stared silently.

"Of course, those two agents were you and Sarah ... before I lost contact with you."

"Before Dragnorr did something to erase our memories, you mean!" Gordon snapped.

"Well, before he erased your existence in normal space-time ... My theory is that the memory loss is merely a symptom -- "

"Please, just shut up!"

Gordon began pacing around the room in a high state of agitation. He paced around for several circuits and came back to face Hylrada.

"Can I send Sarah's Transporter to get you? I mean, we really need some help here, Hylrada. And, it seems you're all there is."

"Oh no, I couldn't do that."

"You mean we can't send the Transporter on a pre-fixed coordinate to you?"

"Oh, that part can be done quite easily."

"Then, come and help Sarah!"

Hylrada hung his head a moment. "I really wish I could. But, you see, time traveling is illegal in my society."

"What?"

"Yes. I could be jailed for life for doing it."

"But you communicate through space and time with us and your other contacts."

"Well, talking is one thing. I do research too. And monitoring, I told you that. That's all fine with the ruling authorities on my world ... but actually traveling through time -- it's forbidden. That's one reason I sent you my Transporters -- so I wouldn't even be tempted any more."

"We need you!"

"Let me tell you of my initial experiments. I performed them in secret, you see. My curiosity got the better of me, and I thought I might actually try it myself if I could perfect a transporter."

"Go on."

"I started small. I used my pet rog and placed a sensor around his neck so it would record his travel and I could determine how well the transporter worked."

"What's a rog?" Gordon asked.

"A rog is a domesticated animal on our world." Hylrada paused. "They are similar to dogs on Earth in shape and demeanor, more or less, except they have four tails."

"I can't quite picture that," Gordon said. "Four tails, you say? I guess they can create quite a breeze when they're happy."

"We have a saying -- 'A happy rog can beat you to death!'"

"Okay, get on with it."

"Well, first I sent Happy, that's his name you know. First, I sent Happy back in time about twenty years in my world's timeline. It all worked fine, and the transporter sent him back after an hour."

"That doesn't sound so bad."

"Well, then I had some trouble with the device that sets the chronometer navigation. I pre-set several settings so Happy would travel to one spot and then another and come back and then travel forward and come back and then back again ... " Hylrada shook his head and sighed.

"What happened?" Gordon sat down and

146

watched Hylrada closely.

"The Transporter left and seemingly seconds later came back. I checked the sensor log, but I got too fast with things. I decided to send him back and forth and back several times in a row."

"And ... "

"Suddenly, three identical Transporters appeared in my lab. The doors to all opened, and out trotted three completely identical rogs. All three of them my Happy."

"What happened then?" Gordon asked.

"They do what rogs always do when they meet another rog. They approached each other and touched noses." Hylrada rolled his eyes and lowered his head into his hands in obvious distress.

"What happened then?" Gordon demanded.

"They exploded."

"*What?*"

"It was terrible. I had nightmares about it for weeks." Hylrada looked up. "You can imagine the mess all over the floor and walls."

Gordon's eyes widened. "What about the three Transporters?"

"As soon as they appeared, the entire area around them became unstable! Why, even the very air trembled and tiny bolts of electricity crackled around them."

"And ... "

"They exploded right after the rogs." Hylrada shook his head. "My lab was completely destroyed." He sighed. "You see, the physics of our universe don't allow for multiple original entities to exist in the same place in space-time -- it's just not ... right."

147

"You never tried again?"

"I've conducted more experiments, yes. I even got to the point where I was going to break the law and travel myself." Hylrada shrugged. "Okay, I did break the law a couple of times. But then I stopped."

"What stopped you?"

"I met you and Sarah. You were in trouble and I helped you out of some tight spots. And then, when Dragnorr crossed your path and destroyed your human-made Transporter -- well, I sent you both of mine."

Gordon took a deep breath.

"So, you're telling me that this Temporal Authority doesn't exist?" Gordon asked.

"Only in our wildest imaginations." Hylrada smiled ruefully.

"The other research contacts ... "

"Some are purely scientists from other worlds in this field of temporal research that I've met via temporal communications, others are ... shall we say ... experimenters ... more like you and I."

"But, there are no reinforcements."

"I'm afraid not."

"Why didn't you tell me this before?"

"You were already depressed by the fact you don't really exist. I didn't want to tell you that, well, we're in this alone."

"I've got to rescue Sarah. She's my only friend. She's my ... " Gordon stood up resolutely and grabbed his Stunner. He looked into Hylrada's eyes.

"Don't go running blindly after her -- that's what Dragnorr wants you to do. We've got to plan."

"We don't have time for that!" Gordon shouted

148

angrily.

"I have an idea. The Time Rods you took from the Anon."

"What about them?" Gordon asked.

"Do they have controls?"

Gordon picked up one and examined it. He found a small keypad and held it up to the screen for Hylrada to examine.

"Yes, although the randomizer setting is active, there is a way to override it and specify a setting." Hylrada turned to other screens and began typing. "I will send you the commands for you to enter on the keypad. Use it to send the other Time Rod to the setting I will specify, which will be to me."

"What are you going to do with a Time Rod?"

"I'm not sure right now, but I may be able to use it to help you somehow," Hylrada suggested.

"Any kind of help is better than nothing." Gordon shook his head.

"Is there anyone else in that time willing to help you too?" Hylrada asked.

"Who would that be? Shakespeare?"

"Here, I am downloading some instructions that will enhance our repairs on the main communicator. Perform them quickly, and I will be able to control some of the Time Transporter's systems remotely."

Gordon glanced at the instructions that filled a secondary screen. He immediately began to take off the cover to the console and start repairs.

He glanced down toward the bottom of the instructions.

"You want me to make these modifications on the Chrono-Nav too? Won't that link your communicator to our Nav systems?"

"Absolutely. Have you thought of anyone who might be willing to assist you in the rescue?"

"I have no idea. Young Tom Walker? He's just a kid. Who would be willing to take on Dragnorr and his band of Shadows and Anon in a night fight? And what weapons could they use against them?"

"Ask William Shakespeare. After all, he is a genius for all ages -- and quite resourceful, just like you. He and his company have a plethora of swords, daggers, rapiers and knives. In fact, the only people allowed weapons within the city of London during this age are soldiers and acting companies ... "

"Actors ... and a playwright? How much good would they be in a rescue? I think Tom might be of better use to me."

"You might be surprised ... "

Chapter Sixteen

"Pretty, pretty Sarah Nightingale."

Dragnorr's shiny black arm reached for Sarah. The black creature gently caressed her face with the back of his curved talon.

Sarah shivered at his icy touch.

"What do you want with me?" she shouted angrily.

"Now, now, Sarah. You have so much anger inside." Dragnorr hissed soothingly. "Can't we be friends?"

"What?" Sarah turned her face away so his talon no longer touched her cheek.

"You are so pretty, my dear. I adore your wheat-colored hair and blue eyes. And your face ... so trusting, so pure."

"I'll never trust you!"

Dragnorr laughed.

Sarah tried to get a good look at his face, but in the darkness of this chamber she could not make out any of his features.

She took in her surroundings quickly as Dragnorr walked around her.

The walls were made of huge blocks of ancient stone, and the air was damp. She surmised she must be in some kind of dungeon or some lower floor of an ancient building.

Suddenly, Dragnorr lifted the hood off his face.

Sarah screamed.

He was hideous.

Two red eyes blazed out of an oblong face. Dragnorr didn't have skin -- the black shininess of his head and neck made her think of some kind of insect. She knew in an instant she was right -- whether it was some memory buried deep inside or not she didn't know.

Yes, Dragnorr was an insectoid, his body covered by a black exoskeleton. As she forced herself to watch, she noted the two huge mandibles that clicked together excitedly at the bottom of his oblong head.

Dragnorr's red eyes blazed.

"Join me, Sarah Nightingale. Together, we will travel time. All worlds, all ages, will be ours for the taking."

"Never!" Sarah shouted.

"It would be so fun. Together, you and I. We could even become more than ... friends!"

"You're not my type, Dragnorr. In fact, you're not even my species!" Sarah felt a shudder of revulsion at the mere thought. "Forget about it!"

"What, you choose this Gordon Smith over me? I have already defeated him once ... and you. I will do it again. And now that I finally have you, it will be so much easier this time."

"Gordon will rescue me! He's done it many times." Sarah smiled confidently.

"I'm counting on it." Dragnorr hissed vehemently.

"What do you mean?"

"I want Gordon Smith to come and 'try' to rescue you. In fact, I've sent one of my couriers to let him know where I've taken you."

"It's a trap then," Sarah whispered.

"Yes!" Dragnorr's mandibles clicked together

152

excitedly.

"You'll find that Gordon and I don't go down quite that easily," Sarah shot back.

"Oh, I know that well enough. That's why I've constructed this particular trap most carefully. I know he will come for you without hesitation. After all, you are his entire world now ... " Dragnorr laughed as she closed her eyes, knowing he was right.

"But, there are too many of us waiting. I have two entire flocks of Shadows waiting for his puny attempt. In addition, I have seven Anons here in reserve. And even if Gordon somehow manages to get through all of them, he still has me to deal with! And I'll be waiting here with my talons around your pretty neck!"

"Gordon will find a way -- just you wait!"

Dragnorr clicked his mandibles together twice.

"You're not as smart as you seem to think you are. We will defeat you once again!" Sarah held her head up proudly. Somehow, in the recesses of her memory, she knew that she and Gordon had defeated Dragnorr several times.

"How many times have you defeated me?" Dragnorr hissed coolly.

Sarah remained silent.

"Ah, you seem perplexed. Could it be you don't ... *remember*." Dragnorr again took the back of his talon and caressed her cheek.

She grimaced under its icy touch.

"I thought I had destroyed and you and Gordon Smith completely the last time. And yet, this twisted temporal side-effect is quite humorous." Dragnorr laughed with a hissing tone. "It seems I have more than one advantage this encounter, Sarah, and I will use that advantage to make this trap work perfectly! And, even if he somehow makes it to this room ... "

"Gordon will find a way to beat you!"

Dragnorr laughed. He turned to leave, but as he approached the only door that led to this dark room, he turned and hissed ominously before he spoke.

"Not this time, Sarah Nightingale. I've realized that although I successfully destroyed you and Gordon in space-time, I must now destroy you here in the ether between space and time. And, if I cannot do that, I will send each of you off alone -- without a Time Transporter -- each to opposite ends of time -- never to see each other again!"

Chapter Seventeen

"I need your help."

Gordon looked deeply into Shakespeare's eyes. He had just explained the entire situation in detail, including the descriptions of the foes they would battle in the darkness.

Tom Walker whistled.

Kempe and Burbage sat in stony silence, their eyes far off in thought.

Gordon figured it was his descriptions of the Shadows and the Anon that had them all sitting there in silent wonder -- or fear. He doubted they had the stomach for a deed like this.

"They sound like a terrible enemy -- more like fighting monsters from a nightmare than battling a real opponent of flesh and blood," Shakespeare mused out loud.

"Will our swords be of any use?" Burbage asked as he rubbed his chin.

"Yes," Gordon said. "They won't hurt them, but the force of the blow will knock them away. And if you strike them just right, you can daze them."

"Where would we need to strike?" Kempe sat forward.

"Right between their eyes."

"How long would they be out of action?" Shakespeare asked.

"Five minutes, ten at the most. After they regain their senses, they'd join the attack again."

"We must be swift then," Shakespeare said. "We must strike quickly, deliver our blows, and get Miss Nightingale out of there."

"Dragnorr will be expecting me." Gordon looked around at the three men and the boy. "But he may not be expecting my bringing along allies."

"We must use that to our advantage," Burbage said.

"We must plan out our rescue. We must use our keen intelligence as another advantage," Shakespeare added.

"Agreed. We must do the unexpected -- that will throw Dragnorr off even more." Gordon smiled confidently.

"Where is she?" Kempe asked.

"That is the problem; I don't know where he's taken her." Gordon shook his head.

"Actually, we might."

Everyone turned to young Tom Walker.

He reached inside his shirt and pulled out an envelope.

"Where did you get that?" Gordon asked.

"Delivered about an hour ago -- you launched right into your plans for the rescue, so I forgot it till just now."

Gordon grabbed it and tore it open. The handwriting seemed oddly familiar -- in an instant, he knew it was Dragnorr's. And yet, it immediately struck him that he'd never seen Dragnorr's handwriting before -- not that he could remember ... clearly.

"It's from Dragnorr!" Gordon exclaimed.

"What does it say?" Burbage stepped next to Gordon and read the note.

"Sarah is my prisoner at the ruins of the Thames battlements. During the darkest hours just before

156

dawn, I will do away with her. Come to me, Gordon Smith, so we may fight one last time. Only if you defeat me, can you hope to save her."

Gordon crumpled the note into a ball and threw it to the ground.

"He wants you to rescue her," Shakespeare said confidently.

"Yes," Gordon said.

"Then, it is a trap." Burbage walked over to a window and stared out.

"Where is this place? I've never heard of it." Gordon asked.

"Farther east, some of the oldest wall defenses built to protect London from attack -- older even than the Tower of London. In fact, the White Tower replaced them as the city's primary defense from any attack launched from the sea up the Thames." Shakespeare finished speaking and walked over to the window to stand beside Richard Burbage.

"They're in ruins now, have been for several centuries." Shakespeare said as he stared out the window.

"Can we get a layout of them? Any old diagrams?" Gordon asked.

"The upper walls are a jumble of stones. However, the lower levels are intact, but there will be passages and rooms underground, all designed for the advantage of the defenders."

"Yes, if once the walls and towers were taken, the defenders would retreat underground for their last stand. And, it was designed so they could hold out until help arrived to seal the breach." Kempe nodded. "It will not be easy."

"But, it's in ruins," Gordon countered.

"Fortresses of stone last for ages, unless torn down. The underground part will be mostly intact," Kempe said.

"Do we have a layout?" Gordon looked from one man to the other.

"No," Burbage said at last.

Gordon sighed.

"But, I know them!" Tom Walker said excitedly.

"What?" the four men said as one.

"I know them like the back of my hand. I played there as a young boy -- all us boys played there, running deep inside them.."

"I've been down them as well," Kempe added. "Since it is in ruins, no one cares if children play among the stones and empty passages or anyone else steps down into them to have a look."

Gordon raised his eyebrows in amazement. In his mind, the truth of Hylrada's words struck home. Perhaps these men were only actors, but the more he talked with them, the more real their help became.

"There is more than one entrance." Tom's eyes twinkled.

"Indeed," Kempe said eagerly. "I would imagine this Dragnorr expects Gordon to attempt his rescue by the entrance where the main tower once stood. It was the main entrance to the underground battlements."

"Right," Tom said as he jumped right before Gordon. "That is the most well-known, but there are two others farther along the ruins."

Tom took his finger and used it to draw an

imaginary line on the table as he continued.

"My friends and I like to use an entrance near a jumble of stones between two shops. It's about a fifteen-minute walk from the main ruins of the big tower. Old folks say the stones used to be a smaller tower and a wall once connected it with the big one. But, the small tower was torn down long ago and now only shops and houses are there -- and a few piles of stones here and there where the wall once stood."

Burbage's eyes lit up. "It can be our back door then."

"The other entrance we know about is right along the river -- they said it was built so that reinforcements arriving inland from the Thames could go straight and quick to the main tower and the outer wall. You'll find it near two working docks. There's an opening in the middle of a pile of big rocks that leads down to a main passage."

"Brilliant!" Gordon felt their sudden enthusiasm energizing his spirit. "I will make my approach by the obvious entrance at the tower's ruins."

"Dragnorr will be expecting that will be the only way you will know," Shakespeare said knowingly. "And he may suspect at least one of us may help you."

"But, with two of you coming up by the other entrances -- we will have the element of surprise." Gordon chuckled.

"Aye!" Tom shouted. "I can lead two of you to the other entrances and point you the right way."

"You'll need to stay with Kempe," Gordon said. "You two will take the entrance by the shops after

159

you show Burbage the entrance by the river."

"We have the beginning of a plan!" Kempe laughed.

Everyone nodded agreement.

"Gentlemen, let us focus our minds upon this dark task." Shakespeare smiled. "We must utilize our knowledge of the enemy and his defenses, and then with our intellect we must carefully plan our every advantage. It is this more than our skill with the sword that will ensure our success!"

Chapter Eighteen

In the darkness, the remnants of a once mighty tower rose from a jumble of large, cut stones strewn along the ground.

In his mind, Gordon could picture the stones all put back together to form a powerful tower that once stood proud in defense of an older London. But only a vague shadow of that tower and protective wall remained. Only the base was intact now -- rising almost twenty feet high.

And plainly visible was the single, darkened entrance.

Gordon held a torch higher against the dark of night.

"It should be almost three in the morning by now," Shakespeare whispered.

"It is time."

Gordon waved the torch and walked forward.

Shakespeare grabbed Gordon by his arm and held him firmly in place.

"What?" Gordon whispered.

"I see movement in the air above the ruins."

Gordon peered intently as he held the torch higher.

Staring, he could barely make out a hint of movement flying through the darkness. But now and then, a sudden dark shape covered the stars for a fleeting moment. He looked harder and saw more of the dark shapes as they flew briefly in front of the brighter stars.

He now strained his ears to hear above the slight breeze that blew from the north.

And when he filtered out even that subtle whispering, the familiar fluttering of large, leathery wings became discernable just above the sigh of the wind.

"Yes, they're waiting for us," Gordon said with a measure of apprehension.

"And there!" Shakespeare pointed to a pile of stones off to their right.

In a split second, a hooded figure ducked out of sight.

"The Anon are here too. There are probably more of them below in the dark corridors of the ruins." Gordon shook his head. "And Shadows too."

Shakespeare patted a sheathed dagger on his waist with one hand as he held up a stout staff in his other hand. "Let us move forward while our hearts are still bold with courage. If we hesitate too long, the fear that lies within us all may dismay us from our task."

"I'm glad we found those staffs in the cache of weapons your company uses for its staged battles. I think those will be of better use to us against these dark forces than the flat blade of a sword." Gordon smiled grimly as he moved forward with two Stunners strapped to his waist.

They stepped toward the remnants of the base and up to the entrance. Gordon pulled a Stunner out and leaned inside. He surveyed the dark interior that was open to the starry sky above.

But no attack came.

As he stepped inside, he noticed an opening in the very middle of the floor. He moved toward the opening and saw stone steps that led down into the ground. As he got closer, he realized it was a spiral staircase -- and so narrow that even a single man would have to walk down them twisting his body sideways.

He held the torch forward as he stepped down -- below him the stone steps spiraled downward into the dense darkness below.

He could see nothing beyond the next spiral.

Down they descended one cautious step at a time.

Gordon waved the torch from side to side as he walked lower. He felt a growing sensation of claustrophobia within the narrow confines of the passage. But he fought this fear too and continued down the seemingly endless spiral steps.

Gordon felt his heart beating harder as he prepared himself for the coming confrontation.

Finally, they reached a level stone floor.

As they stepped out he waved his torch with broad sweeping motions -- as if to frighten any waiting Shadows away.

The flickering light revealed no enemies -- only a long corridor.

A single corridor lined with ancient stone stretched before them. And in the far, far distance, the stones of the corridor grew smaller until the walls, floor and ceiling blended into the darkness.

The corridor seemed to stretch on into infinity.

"It's like a nightmare -- except we're awake!" Shakespeare murmured.

Somewhere far down the corridor, a Shadow shrieked -- its eerie cry echoing weirdly until it grew fainter and fainter and gradually faded to nothing.

"Oh, it's going to get better than that," Gordon whispered.

They moved forward and saw a doorway between the stones a few steps to their right. Gordon held the torch higher. There were more darkened doorways on either side farther up the corridor.

"They could attack us from any of them as we walk by," Shakespeare said.

"Or from behind," Gordon whispered.

Gordon felt and heard Shakespeare turn around.

"You keep an eye for the rear, and I'll keep an eye out ahead. Keep that staff ready to strike," Gordon whispered.

"I am ready."

They moved forward carefully.

Reaching the first doorway, Gordon took a sudden step forward and waved the torch as he pointed his Stunner inside.

Nothing.

Gordon's heart pounded like a jackhammer now.

As he started to walk forward, he saw a piece of paper nailed to the wall. He held the torch up to it.

"There's a note."

Shakespeare turned his head slightly and glanced at it but quickly turned back to face the darkness behind them.

"What does it say?"

"We are waiting for you, Gordon Smith. You must know this is a trap. And yet, if you do not come for your precious Sarah, I promise that you will never see her again."

"It is a trap." Shakespeare's staff wavered in his hand.

"He knew that I would know -- of this I am sure. But, did he know that I would assume that he would know and plan with that foreknowledge?"

Shakespeare shook his head profoundly.

They moved forward.

Gordon felt the hairs on the back of his neck rising. He could sense something was about to happen.

He kept his eyes locked on the next darkened doorway, his Stunner pointed right at it in anticipation of an attack.

Suddenly, Shakespeare shouted behind him.

Gordon glanced quickly back over his shoulder.

In the darkness of the corridor he could just make out the movement of Shadows flying rapidly towards them out of the darkness.

"Swing your staff, Shakespeare! Aim for their ugly faces!" Gordon shouted as he turned back.

An Anon leaped at him.

Gordon fired, and the stunned Anon fell into him and knocked him against the hard stone wall. He grunted as he shoved the limp figure away.

Shadows shrieked from every direction, and the eerie echoes bouncing off the stones sent a shiver through his body.

Gordon fired again and again, and Shadows fell all around his feet.

"Help!"

Gordon turned and discovered Shakespeare on the ground covered by writhing Shadows.

He fired once, waited as one curled its wings

and fell off, and fired again.

Shakespeare rose to a sitting position and wielded his staff with blow after blow, knocking new attackers from the air.

Gordon turned back and suddenly was forced against the hard stones.

Two Shadows latched onto him with their tiny, vise-like claws.

One grabbed him around his neck while it flapped its leather wings against his shoulders in an attempt to get him off-balance. The other grabbed his left leg and flapped its wings rapidly as well.

Gordon stunned the one on his leg and used his torch to strike the other on its back.

It shrieked terribly and released its grip.

Suddenly, the corridor was filled with Shadows flying at them from both directions.

Gordon aimed, but his Stunner clicked -- it was empty. He quickly holstered it while he waved his torch back and forth. He pulled the other and began firing.

"I can't hold them!" Shakespeare shouted. "There's too many!"

Gordon turned back and fired three times. He turned back forward and fired non-stop.

But more Shadows kept flying out of the darkness, replacing the others that lay stunned around their feet.

"Over here!"

Gordon ran toward another doorway where he'd anticipated the attack would come from. Though he stunned the Shadows that flew between him and it, the dark corridor still filled with flying movement beyond.

"William! Follow me!" Gordon shouted.

Shakespeare twirled his staff and knocked first one and then another attacker back. He turned and ran toward Gordon and the side room.

Gordon covered him with fire, and after Shakespeare ran inside he followed.

They were trapped!

The room had no other exits.

"Take your stand at the door while I reload!" Gordon dumped the empty cartridge and slammed another into place.

Meanwhile, Shakespeare stood just inside the doorway and struck again and again at the shrieking Shadows fighting to gain entrance and overwhelm them.

Gordon holstered the loaded Stunner and then pulled the other Stunner and replaced its cartridge. Shakespeare shouted as the shrieks from the Shadows grew to a crescendo. Gordon aimed just as Shakespeare's staff flew out of his grasp; the playwright fell backward with four Shadows latched onto him.

Gordon fired, knocking one off.

But then, three Shadows slammed into him. One grasped his right arm, fighting to keep him from taking aim, while another grabbed his left arm.

The torch fell from his grasp to the floor.

Gordon fell backwards as another and another grabbed him.

He fell onto the floor covered with the shrieking monsters -- two more grabbed his right arm, and he felt his grasp on his Stunner weakening.

"William! Kick them off -- hit them! Anything! Don't let them pin you down!" Gordon shouted.

"Alas, Gordon! I cannot move," Shakespeare shouted back.

In that moment, he felt the Stunner knocked from his hand as he too was pinned fast.

He looked up.

The darkness seethed with Shadows.

Gordon felt his heart sinking into defeat ...

Chapter Nineteen

"Back I say! Back!"

Gordon looked over at Shakespeare lying on the ground. Both men were covered with dark, moving shapes while the air above them grew thick with flying movement.

"It's Kempe!" Shakespeare whispered.

A chorus of shrieks erupted all around them.

"Swing, man! Swing harder!"

"That's Burbage!" Shakespeare shouted with a hearty voice.

The shrieks grew deafening, and Gordon felt some of the Shadows lift off him back into the air.

He shook himself and got his left arm free. He quickly pulled his other Stunner from its holster and fired.

Shadow after Shadow fell off until he was free.

He jumped up and fired at the ones holding Shakespeare down.

Seconds later, Kempe, Burbage and Tom ran inside. The two men each wielded a short club in one hand while they waved torches with the other. And even young Tom swung out with vigor and struck the Shadows soundly, making them cry out in anger as they fell to the ground.

"Quick. Get up!" Burbage shouted urgently.

Gordon grabbed his torch and did a quick scan of the floor. He found Shakespeare's staff and kicked it toward him. His other Stunner, however, was gone, probably taken by a Shadow.

They ran out into the corridor, and young Tom Walker led the way deeper into the underground ruins.

In the distance, they saw retreating shapes disappearing into the darkness beyond their torchlight. Behind them, they heard the sound of many wings growing fainter with each passing moment.

"We've beaten them off." Kempe laughed.

"They'll quickly regroup," Gordon said, panting. "We've got to find Sarah before they attack again."

"And we mustn't let them trap us in a room with but one exit!" Shakespeare added.

They ran faster.

"Tom, where are you leading us?" Gordon asked.

"I'm just running!"

They all ran a few steps more.

"All right, hold up."

They all came to a halt. The four men and the boy each held their torch high to light up as much of the area as possible while each held his weapon at the ready.

They leaned against the cool stones as they all rested and to catch their breath. Several moments went by with only the sound of their rapid breathing.

"I'm glad you ran in the right direction," Gordon said after he caught his breath.

"Sure. I figured you didn't want to go back the way you came in," Tom replied.

"Right then, what's on down that way?"

Tom looked down the darkened corridor.

"We'll come to the side entrances we used to enter here. And then beyond them, there's a big open place with a dirt floor. And there's lots of broken crates and junk there too."

"A big store room?" Burbage asked.

"Sounds like it," Shakespeare said.

"And beyond that room?" Gordon asked.

"There are a few side rooms, but the corridor ends there. Where it would continue, it's all blocked up now."

"Dragnorr must have Sarah there." Gordon readied himself.

Without warning, several black arms suddenly reached out between the stones and grabbed his arms.

Shouts echoed as each person found himself caught by tiny claws reaching from between the cracks in the stones.

Gordon realized in an instant that if the Shadows could squeeze their bodies between the cracks of wooden walls, they could squeeze between cracks of stone walls too.

Tom screamed as he dropped his club and fought back.

Gordon felt more claws reaching for his legs as the Shadows tried to pull him up against the stone wall and pin him tight. He knew once they had them pinned ...

From out of the darkness, the sound of running footsteps echoed.

"The Anon are coming!" Gordon cried out.

He now increased his efforts, kicking and thrashing at the tiny claws grasping at him from between the stones. He twisted his body in an effort to reach his holstered Stunner.

171

He twirled the torch until the flames were pointing at the ground. He pushed the fire against one of the arms and heard a shriek as it released its grip.

He stabbed with the torch again, and two more yelled with pain as the arms disappeared back between the stones.

"Use your torches, lads!"

Everyone now twisted and waved their torches against the wall and the reaching arms. More shrieks erupted and more arms disappeared.

Now, everyone kicked and jumped until they freed themselves enough to use their clubs or staffs or Stunner.

The shrieks reached a terrible crescendo of pain as the five leapt into the center of the corridor and away from the walls, where more arms appeared reaching urgently to grab them.

"What sort of monsters are they?" Burbage asked as he rubbed the dozens of tiny scratch wounds on his arms.

"They're not of this world!" Kempe declared.

"No, they're not of Earth," Gordon agreed as he too rubbed the nasty scratches that covered his arms. "They're not of this time either. They're alien creatures that live in the ether between space and time."

"What?" they asked all together.

"They're like hounds, except they can fly. And their bodies are not flesh and blood; they can squeeze themselves between tiny cracks in wood or stone." Gordon let out a big breath of relief.

"Flying hounds?" Burbage asked.

"No, flying monkeys. Gordon told us the other night," Shakespeare added.

"Nasty buggers," Gordon said. "Wings that are strong enough to hurt, arms and legs tipped with claws -- and you can't quite see them, no matter how hard you look. Somehow, their black skin absorbs light."

"But they hate light?" Kempe asked.

"Yes. And blows to their head will daze them."

Gordon suddenly remembered the footsteps and jumped forward with his torch.

At the edge of the light, a group of cloaked figures stood. Now with the light upon them, they quickly retreated back into the darkness.

"They don't have faces!" Tom Walker shouted in surprise.

"No -- only a smooth silver skin with black lines crisscrossing where a face should be." Gordon walked forward with his torch, but the Anon retreated rapidly now.

"Let's move, before they regroup and attack again."

Gordon led the group forward. They continued waving their torches, especially as they approached another darkened doorway. But everything was dark and silent except for the soft tread of their footsteps.

They continued down the dark corridor for several minutes without incident.

"Careful, lads. I can almost feel the Shadows coming for us," Gordon whispered as they approached another doorway.

Gordon pressed himself against the stone wall opposite it. The others followed suit as they held their torches toward it to lighten its interior and reveal any potential attackers.

Suddenly, dozens of wriggling arms erupted from the cracks in the stone walls all around him and wild shrieks filled the air.

The claw-tipped hands reached urgently for him as he stood frozen staring at them. They reached closer until one latched onto his arm. He shook it free and jumped to the other side of the corridor.

He glanced over as the others screamed in shocked surprise. They too stared at the arms reaching out from between the cracks in the walls all around them, sightlessly reaching for them. And just as he had done, everyone jumped over to the other side.

"It's those flying monkeys again!" Burbage shouted.

Black arms erupted from the walls behind them -- wriggling and reaching for them like claw-tipped snakes.

Gordon and the others screamed louder as they felt the claws grab them and pull them against the wall.

"Strike them! Don't let them hold you!" Gordon shouted as he slammed his torch against the arms holding him. Over and over he struck, but as one claw let go, another grabbed him again.

Gordon fought harder.

The others used their torches or clubs or staff -- whatever they held in their free arm, and struck at the claws. And like Gordon, as they knocked one claw away, several others shot out at them.

Their shouts and screams rose higher as the

walls filled with reaching claws.

"Jump to the middle!" Gordon slammed his torch into the last claw holding him and jumped right into the middle of the corridor.

The others struck again and again until they too freed themselves and joined Gordon.

As he looked around, the walls were alive with reaching, twisting arms from both walls. But since they stood directly in the center, none could quite reach them.

All at once, the arms disappeared back between the stones.

Gordon bent over, panting with his exertions and his fright.

"Well now, that was quite a shock! They must be very fast!" Kempe shook his head in wonder.

"All right, we go right down the center. Stay away from the walls -- they're going to try and grab us again if they can."

"Lovely," Kempe said with a sarcastic tone.

They walked single file down the long corridor, each keeping a sharp eye on the walls. No one said a word now as they walked with their torches and weapons at the ready.

And from time to time, one or more of them would jump with surprise when another set of twisting claws suddenly erupted from the cracks in the walls -- claws reaching for them.

"I say, this is really too much like a nightmare!" Shakespeare waved his torch at two more claws that suddenly appeared, reaching for his neck.

"Here's where we came in."

Gordon glanced back. He was ahead of them

again.

Tom pointed at two side corridors.

When he had walked by, after waving his torch at them to make sure nothing was ready to attack from within, he had simply discounted them as another set of rooms.

"We can retreat by way of one of them once we rescue Sarah. They're closer than the one Shakespeare and I used," Gordon said matter-of-factly. "How far to the big room?"

"It's just ahead," Tom replied.

Indeed, after a few more minutes, they found themselves inside what seemed like a huge cavern.

Gordon took a step and realized the next moment that there were no longer any walls on either side of him now. He stopped immediately and held his torch up as high as possible.

The room was vast.

As they all gathered around and raised their torches together, the combined light did not illuminate even a fourth of the cavernous room.

"All right, which way?" Shakespeare asked.

Gordon continued to stare around the room. Something had caught his eye -- movement.

As he focused, he realized the room was alive with movement inside the darkness just out of the reach of their flickering light.

"They're all here." Gordon felt dismay fill his heart.

"I see them!" Burbage said with surprise. "The darkness is full of movement!"

"And when we get out there in the middle, they'll attack us from all sides," Kempe said with defeat.

"Welcome, Gordon Smith."

Gordon turned to the hissing voice. It came directly across from them on the other side of the room still enveloped in total darkness.

"Aye, Dragnorr. I've not come to talk tonight," Gordon said with a challenge.

"I would expect nothing less from my old nemesis."

"Where is she?"

"She is here as my prisoner, but I tire of her."

"Release her, Dragnorr!"

"No, you must come and get her -- if you want to see her again! Otherwise, I will dispose of her."

Gordon glanced at each of the men and at the boy.

Each nodded back at him.

They all charged, screaming at the top of their voices.

"Will the screams frighten them?" Tom asked between screams.

"Probably not, but it makes me feel braver!" Gordon replied between his own screams.

They all screamed louder as they waved their torches and weapons at the movement in the darkness all around them.

As they reached the very middle of the vast room, the combined Shadows attacked them from every direction.

Their shrieks were deafening, reverberating around the room over and over all around them until their heads spun.

The five stopped in their tracks, waving their

torches and weapons.

Gordon fired volley after volley from his Stunner.

But there were too many.

A Shadow grabbed Kempe's torch and flew off with it. Two others wrestled the club out of Burbage's hand as he fought back with his torch.

And five leaped on Tom's back and flapped their wings furiously as they dragged him off into the darkness.

"Help me!" Tom cried.

Gordon fired twice, dropping two of them.

And then his weapon clicked empty.

He raced forward waving his torch as the three remaining Shadows shrieked at him with black fangs bared.

"Gordon, are you there?"

Gordon recognized Hylrada's voice in his earpiece communicator.

"Hylrada? Is that you?"

"Yes, I've made some enhancements, and I am now able to communicate to you via the console in your Transporter forwarded over to your earpiece."

"I'm a little busy at the moment!"

Gordon punched one of the Shadows with his Stunner and slammed the fire of his torch against three more who tried to grab him from out of the darkness.

"Well, I thought I might be of help to you," Hylrada said in a calm tone.

"Help! We'll take any you can give us!" Gordon shouted as he kicked the last Shadow off Tom and then sank to the ground under the weight of four

Shadows who fell upon him.

"Help!" Gordon shouted again.

"Yes, let's see ... I'm reading the coordinates now ... Yes ... spatial coordinates completed."

Gordon writhed on the ground as more and more of the Shadows fell upon him with shrieks of delight. He glanced over and realized that everyone else was now on the ground as the Shadows attacked en masse.

He realized with dread that they were going to lose.

"Hylrada!" Gordon fought harder as he felt the tiny claws pinning him against the ground.

"Ah yes, there you are. Let me try this first."

Suddenly, a single light appeared in the midst of the darkness.

All movement in the room stopped at once as everyone stared at the new intruder.

"What's *that*?" Shakespeare shouted.

An animal that resembled a greyhound with a large hump on its shoulders stood wagging its four tails. The dirt on the floor flew up under the steady breeze of the wagging members.

"It's a dog with four tails!" Kempe shouted with surprise.

"No, it's a rog!" Gordon answered.

"A rog? Are you ridding -- I mean kidding?" Kempe asked in disbelief.

"Did my rog appear in good order?" Hylrada asked.

"Yes!

"Good. Well the Time Rod worked, correctly integrated with my console."

179

"Get them!" Dragnorr shouted from the darkness. "Take them now!"

All at once, the Shadows pressed home their attack.

Suddenly, a bar of light appeared above the melee.

Once again, all movement ceased as everyone looked up.

In the next instant, bright lights erupted in a myriad of explosions that lit up the entire room like flashes of lightning.

"Fireworks?" Gordon asked.

"Yes, Gordon. The Shadows hate light. As well as the Anon. And I just happened to have a supply ..."

The erupting blossoms of light mixed with colored sparks suddenly erupted again with a long string of loud explosions.

The Shadows shrieked in despair as they covered their faces with their claws and flew up into the air.

But they flew directly into the midst of the exploding lights in their blinded condition.

Their shrieks reached a fever pitch as they all flew toward the far walls and disappeared between the cracks.

Gordon looked around.

At the edge of the room, a dozen Anon covered themselves with their black cloaks and disappeared in a flash. Gordon knew they had just jumped away via their own Time Transporters.

As he stood up, the huge room was completely empty.

Gordon picked up a torch as the fireworks slowly died down and the darkness began to return.

"Get up!" Gordon urged. "The Anon have left -- and I don't think the Shadows will come back for quite some time after that light display."

The others rose and gathered their weapons and torches.

As they gathered around him, Gordon looked over at the wall before him.

In the darkness of the doorway, two glowing red eyes stared ominously at him.

Chapter Twenty

Gordon ran straight for the glowing eyes.

But as he neared, they disappeared. He pointed his Stunner forward and stepped resolutely toward the doorway. He waved his torch inside and jumped inside in a single bound.

He faced two figures.

Uri stood on one side of the room, his eyes wide with surprise.

And on the other side, Sarah sat against the wall, her wrists and ankles bound and her mouth gagged. As he looked, he saw her blue eyes pleading to him as she pointed furiously at Uri.

"What are you doing here?" Shakespeare asked Uri with surprise.

"He brought me here," Uri said simply.

"Who?" Gordon prompted harshly.

"That creature with the red eyes."

"Where is he now?" Gordon shot back.

"He just disappeared."

Gordon nodded his head, realizing Dragnorr must have used his own Transporter to jump away.

Sarah began to grunt furiously as she struggled to get up.

"Hang on, Sarah." Gordon walked toward her as she increased her urgent movements, pointing her bound wrists at something behind him. Gordon looked back in the general direction where she was pointing -- which was at Uri and Shakespeare and Tom

"Kempe, Burbage, you keep an eye outside in case any of the Shadows come back."

The two men placed themselves on either side of the doorway with their torches held high as they kept a sharp eye on the cavernous room outside.

Shakespeare and Tom walked closer to Uri, each carefully looking him over as if something was not quite right.

"Uri, it's quite a surprise to find you here," Shakespeare said.

"Not as surprised as I am to see you and the others." Uri laughed.

Shakespeare turned his head and surveyed him more closely.

"You seem ... fatter than the last time we saw you," Shakespeare said.

"It's the darkness-sss ... " Uri said, with a slight hissing.

Gordon turned back to Sarah, who'd managed to jump up and almost shout her grunts through the gag.

"Hang on, Sarah. You'll hurt yourself -- "

Everything happened all at once.

Gordon heard the voices cry out behind him.

As he turned, both Shakespeare and Tom flew past him through the air.

Gordon stared in shock as a nine-foot tall Dragnorr stood up to his full height. The black creature had his back toward him as he struck at both Kempe and Burbage and knocked them out into the darkened room, sending their torches flying out of their grasps and through the air.

Gordon stood alone facing the giant Dragnorr.

"Where did you ... " Gordon stared down at the skin suit crumpled on the dirt floor.

"Quite the disguise, eh, Gordon?" Dragnorr laughed.

"Uh, quite."

Dragnorr raised his two arms high; the single curved talon that tipped each glistened in the torchlight. He stood on four, spread legs, his elongated body now stretched out to its full length.

"I am very much surprised you defeated my Shadows as easily as you did. I must congratulate you." Dragnorr clicked his mandibles together. "How did you manage to get those fireworks underground like that?"

"Hylrada."

Dragnorr hissed vehemently.

"I tire of this game, Gordon Smith. As soon as I knock that blasted torch out of your hand and put it out, I shall call my Anon back and dispose of you and Sarah once and for all."

"What are you going to do?" Gordon asked. Behind him, he heard Shakespeare groaning, as well as Kempe and Burbage outside, as they came back to their senses.

"You're wasting time, Gordon."

"I thought it was a good question."

Dragnorr attacked.

Gordon jumped aside as he waved his torch at Dragnorr's face.

Dragnorr struck a glancing blow against Gordon's shoulder and sent him flying across the room into a face-first landing.

Gordon spat out a mouthful of dirt as he started to jump back up.

Without warning, the growling rog leaped over

184

his head.

"A *rog*?" Dragnorr shouted angrily.

The rog sank his teeth into one of Dragnorr's legs.

Dragnorr roared in pain.

And then he raised his curved talons and attacked again.

Gordon rolled away just in time as one of Dragnorr's talons stabbed deeply into the ground where he had just lain.

Shakespeare rose up unsteadily and grabbed his staff off the ground. He charged, swinging his weapon.

Dragnorr knocked him away with his arm as he vigorously shook his leg, trying to dislodge the rog.

A club flew through the air and struck Dragnorr squarely on the side of his head.

Dragnorr again shouted with pain as he turned to face Burbage.

"Puny human!" Dragnorr smacked Burbage and sent him flying back out into the darkness of the large room.

"Hylrada! We need more help!" Gordon shouted as he pulled his Stunner and fired.

The shot hit Dragnorr right in the chest and sent him backward several steps.

Dragnorr stood motionless a moment -- dazed. The only movement was his mandibles clicking together. But mere seconds later, his eyes grew focused again.

And he charged right at Gordon.

"Hylrada!"

"Gordon, my readings indicate that is a very

185

small room. I might -- "

"Hylrada! Now!"

"Oh, all right. If you insist."

Dragnorr swung a talon at him.

Gordon jumped back and fired again, hitting Dragnorr right in the face.

Dragnorr roared until the stone walls shook as he stumbled backward a single step. His red eyes unfocused and refocused several times.

"I will kill you for that!"

Gordon aimed and pulled the trigger.

But the Stunner clicked empty.

He held it up and said, "Always at the worst time."

Dragnorr bent his four legs and leaped right at him.

Gordon started to leap aside, but his foot slipped and he fell to his knees. He watched helplessly as Dragnorr flew toward him.

As the huge monster continued through the air, a line of sparkling light appeared right over him.

In the next second, a barrage of multicolored explosions lit up the room with such a blinding intensity that Gordon himself had to cover his eyes.

The acrid smell of burnt gunpowder seared his nostrils inside the small room. Even with his eyes closed the flashes of blinding light hurt, and the explosions rang out so loudly he felt one would surely explode in his face.

And even when he opened his eyes as the explosions and lights finally faded, all he could see for the first few seconds were spots before his eyes.

A heavy object landed right next to him.

Gordon rolled away in the opposite direction as fast as he could in his blinded condition.

Dragnorr screamed out with pain.

In the next moment, he heard Tom Walker cry out.

Gordon blinked rapidly, trying to get rid of the spots and regain his vision. He fumbled in his pocket for another charge to reload his Stunner. His fingers found the familiar object and then, mainly by touch, he ejected the empty and slammed the fresh charge into place.

He heard movement and grunts and then Tom crying out in fear again.

But he couldn't focus enough to see more than blurred movements.

Sarah cried out, but her screams were still muffled by the gag.

Tom's cries stopped suddenly. The rog yelped as Dragnorr kicked it away.

Finally, Gordon made out the figure of Dragnorr against the darkness.

He fired and ran forward.

Dragnorr cried out again as Gordon's shot hit him square in the back.

Finally, Gordon's vision cleared enough so he could make things out.

Dragnorr stood over Sarah with a raised talon as if to hurt her. In one arm, he held Tom Walker captive.

Dragnorr realized Gordon was pointing his freshly loaded Stunner at him.

He shifted Tom before him and used him as a shield as he brought his other talon tight against

Tom's throat.

"Don't come any closer, Gordon, or the boy dies!"

Gordon paused, his Stunner aimed at Dragnorr's head.

"Put it down, or I slash the boy's throat!"

Gordon lowered his Stunner.

The huge monster wavered unsteadily, dazed from both the fireworks and Gordon's direct hits.

Gordon turned his head slightly as he heard the others stumbling to their feet.

"Tell them to stay where they are!" Dragnorr shouted.

"Let the boy go," Gordon said firmly.

Dragnorr looked over at Sarah. He took a step toward her.

Gordon fired at the ground right between Dragnorr and Sarah.

Suddenly, more fireworks began exploding.

Dragnorr screamed as he tried to cover his eyes with a talon.

Gordon aimed his Stunner.

But, Dragnorr backpedaled quickly, still holding Tom before him as a human shield.

Gordon aimed carefully at Dragnorr's' head and tightened his finger on the trigger.

In a flash of light, Dragnorr and Tom disappeared.

"What?" Kempe shouted.

"He's gone," Gordon spat. "He used his Transporter. I should have figured it was in here."

"Transporter? All I saw was a door suddenly appear out of thin air," Shakespeare said in disbelief.

Gordon ran over and quickly untied Sarah.

"Are you all right?" Gordon asked.

She balled her fist and hit him on the arm.

"Ow ... I guess you are."

"Couldn't you tell that was Dragnorr in disguise when you first came in?" she asked with exasperation.

"I was kind of distracted at the time, Sarah dear. After all, my focus was to save you."

Her eyes lit up at his concern. She smiled at him.

"How could they simply disappear like that?" Shakespeare repeated in disbelief.

Sarah jumped up and ran over to the spot where they disappeared. Gordon felt a wave of surprise when she picked up something.

"What is it?" Gordon asked.

Sarah picked up the object and inspected it.

"A data disc."

Chapter Twenty-One

Gordon and Sarah raced through the early morning streets of London.

They had parted with the others back at High Street. Shakespeare, Burbage and Kempe each made their way back to their respective residences for some much needed rest. Their part was over.

But Gordon and Sarah had to rescue young Tom Walker.

The rog trotted along beside them, easily keeping pace.

"What's the name of your rog, Hylrada?" Gordon asked as he ran between two men going in the opposite direction.

"Rawf."

"Oh yes, makes perfect sense -- Rawf the rog."

They passed three women who stared in shock at the rog.

"A new breed, you know! Quite unique with those extra tails!" Gordon shouted over his shoulder with a big smile.

Rawf barked happily.

"What are we going to do?" Sarah asked as she ran beside Gordon.

"I'm not quite sure about that just yet, but I'm sure we'll come up with something."

Sarah groaned.

"The data disc may contain useful information on Dragnorr's whereabouts," Hylrada's voice chimed clearly inside both their earpieces.

"Yes, I hope you're right," Gordon said breathlessly as he and Sara and Rawf ran through a crowd of people.

"When do you estimate arrival at the alley where you left your Time Transporters?" Hylrada asked.

"Here we go now." Gordon paused as an especially large crowd of people on their way to work approached. He looked past them to the entrance of the alley.

"Yes, one more block and then down that alley."

"Excellent. It is imperative that you and Sarah review that disc as quickly as possible and go after Dragnorr."

"Why is that?" Gordon asked.

"I'm afraid that Dragnorr may do something despicable with the child once he decides he is of no further use to him."

"Right! We're on the way now."

Gordon and Sarah weaved through the crowd as fast as they could.

As he neared the alley, Gordon noticed one of the men in a group ahead of him turn and look directly at him.

They locked eyes with each other for a split second.

He gasped.

Gordon recognized him!

But the man's face seemed to blur, as did the other people around him. And then the man ducked down among the others and ran on out of sight.

Gordon felt his heart skip a beat as he lost his breath. He stopped and bent over, gasping for breath. He looked around, but it seemed everything was spinning out of control.

"Gordon, what is it?" Sarah cried out with concern.

He looked up, trying to spot the man again.

"I saw someone up ahead -- someone I know ... "

"Who do you know *here*?" Sarah wondered out loud.

"I'm not really sure; I only just got a look at him. But I felt strongly that I recognized him."

"Oh, Gordon. You couldn't have. Come on, we've got to hurry!"

Sarah grabbed him by his shoulders and pulled him upright.

He stood unsteadily as he brushed himself off. He took a few deep breaths. And as he did so, he happened to glance up.

He felt his heart jump out of his chest.

Or at least, if felt as if it had.

Gordon stared at two figures standing at the window of the third floor of the building directly across from the alley.

It was a man and a woman.

Gordon stared in astonishment a moment as he tried to focus his eyes and make out the details on their faces. They seemed so familiar, and yet ...

Their faces wavered and blurred as if a mist had somehow appeared in the air.

"What? Oh, I see ... *what?*" Sarah whispered in total disbelief.

And in a flash, both figures dropped to the floor out of sight.

Gordon couldn't breathe now, and he suddenly felt as if he were on fire. His heart pounded so hard that his head ached with a massive migraine. He simply felt ... terrible.

"Gordon? Who were they?" Sarah's voice betrayed her panic and fear.

He tried to speak, but although the words were in his mind, somehow he could no longer control his mouth in order to form words -- such a basic skill ... Gone!

As he looked around helplessly, everything in sight suddenly became fluid. The entire world seemed to grow unstable and shudder as if it had suddenly changed into a liquid state bombarded by gigantic, invisible waves.

Gordon forgot about his lost speech and looked around in shock as the world around him rippled in large currents of motion -- folding and undulating. Everything he viewed rolled and surged as if fluid ...

"What is happening?" Hylrada's voice asked in his earpiece.

"I'm ... I'm not sure," Gordon finally managed to say.

He looked up and noticed Sarah staring around with the same shocked expression he was sure was on his face.

"Do you see it too?"

"Yes," Sarah whispered. "The world's changed somehow ... there are waves passing through us ... "

"What's that you say?" Hylrada asked excitedly.

Rawf whined and tucked his tails between his legs.

"Something is wrong," Gordon said. "The world is full of ripples ... like time and space is suddenly

193

fluid around us."

"That can't be good," Hylrada said with obvious concern.

"No, I didn't think so." Gordon stood -- and stumbled -- and finally managed to get up on his feet in spite of the world moving unsteadily around him.

"You'd better hurry. Once you get inside your Transporters, you'll be outside time and space again."

Gordon and Sarah raced forward.

As he turned into the alley, Gordon glanced back at the window.

He saw them peeking at him from behind the curtains.

In that moment, the world rushed at him in large waves like a storm at sea. He took a single step forward, and the very air shimmered as if he had stepped through an invisible curtain rippling with light.

Gordon stepped on through, stumbled badly and fell to the ground.

Sarah screamed and fell beside him as Rawf howled and ran a few steps further on and stopped. The rog whined miserably.

"What was that?" Sarah asked.

"I don't know." Gordon shook his head to ward off the intense dizziness. His vision blurred, and he felt like he was falling.

A strange humming laced with static filled his earpiece -- a sound like an insect almost, except he could barely make out parts of words now and then.

"Hylrada, is that you?" Gordon asked.

The humming and static changed to garbled words. And suddenly, Hylrada's voice could be heard, though only bits and pieces of words were barely discernable.

"not wait ... dannn ... hurry ..."

"Hylrada, we can't hear you. You're breaking up."

Gordon's vision suddenly blurred completely. He shook his head and rubbed his eyes as the light became unbearably bright. But he and Sarah raced forward. Somehow they didn't knock anyone down, though they continuously brushed against other passersby.

The static and humming grew louder ...

They finally made it to the alley. As he turned into it, Gordon glanced back at the window.

He saw them -- the man and the woman -- peeking from behind the curtains.

In that moment, the world rushed in large waves like a storm at sea. He took a single step forward, and the very air shimmered as if he had stepped through an invisible curtain rippling with light.

Déjà vu overwhelmed him.

Gordon stepped on through and stumbled badly. He fell to the ground.

Sarah screamed and fell beside him as Rawf howled and ran a few steps further on and stopped. The rog whined miserably.

"What just happened?" Sarah asked

"I don't know. But it seems we stepped through that wall of light twice in a row somehow!" Gordon shook his head to ward off the intense dizziness.

A strange humming laced with static filled his

earpiece -- a sound like an insect almost, except he could barely make out parts of words now and then.

"Hylrada, is that you?" Gordon asked.

The humming and static changed to garbled words. And suddenly, Hylrada's voice could be heard, though only bits and pieces of words were barely discernable.

"wait lonnn ... dannn ... hurrrrr ... "

"Hylrada, we can't hear you. You're breaking up."

Gordon's vision suddenly blurred completely. He shook his head and rubbed his eyes as the light became unbearably bright.

The static and humming grew louder ... .

Gordon's body jerked involuntarily.

Silence filled his earpiece. In the next moment, Hylrada's voice came through loud and clear.

"Run! Get inside the Transporters!"

Gordon and Sarah stood up at once and ran toward the end of the alley where both their Time Transporters were parked.

But neither he nor Sarah could run in a straight line. In fact, it was all Gordon could do to stay upright with the world around him rippling in waves and his sense of balance compromised by the dizziness inside his mind.

At last, they made it to the end of the alley.

Sarah held up her key and waited.

Nothing happened.

Gordon felt a wave of panic hit him.

He picked up his key and held it up.

A door appeared out of thin air.

"Quick, Sarah, get inside my Transporter."

She ran past him and leapt inside along with Rawf.

Gordon walked back over and held up his key, trying to open the door to Sarah's Transporter.

Nothing happened.

He jabbed blindly with the key, but he couldn't find the door!

It wasn't there.

Another wave enveloped him like a tsunami through space-time.

He lost his balance, got it back, ran over to the door of his Transporter and jumped inside.

The door disappeared.

Inside the Time Transporter, Gordon stared at Sarah as she stared back at him.

"My Transporter's gone!" Sarah said in total shock.

"I know!" Gordon wiped his forehead. "What happened with that?"

"Could it have been stolen?" Sarah asked.

Gordon shook his head and took a breath.

"I'm not sure. Maybe Dragnorr took it. Or one of his Anon." He looked around the interior of his Transporter. To his relief, everything seemed solid with no rippling effect at all. "Everything seems normal in here."

Sarah looked quickly around.

"Yes, no more ripples through time and space in here. And ... I don't feel ill any more."

"Me either." Gordon tapped his chest. "Yes -- head's clear, vision's clear, and I don't feel like I'm going to erupt into spontaneous combustion any second."

197

"Wow, that's pretty ill!" Sarah looked at him with deep concern.

"Could Dragnorr have done something to alter time and space out there?" Sarah asked anxiously. Her sandy blonde hair fell across her cheek as she tilted her head inquisitively.

"Quite probably," Hylrada said clearly in their earpieces.

"What could have happened that would affect everything like that? I mean, everything -- buildings, roads, people, even the sky -- seemed to ripple as if it were all liquid!"

"*Or in a state of temporal flux,*" Hylrada said with a mysterious air.

Gordon and Sarah locked eyes with each other.

"And those two people in the window watching us?" Sarah asked. "It seemed they were expecting us."

"Yes, I got that same feeling when I saw them. It felt like they were there waiting for us." Gordon closed his eyes and rubbed the sides of his head as the memory of the intense migraine flashed again. He hoped with all his heart it would not turn into another knee-buckling headache.

"Perhaps spies for Dragnorr?" Hylrada suggested.

"Maybe he suspected the general area of our Transporters and placed the spies to watch out for us," Sarah added quickly.

"And that other man, I couldn't quite get a fix on him. But deep inside, I knew I'd seen him before."

"Perhaps someone at the pub? Or, one of the men who grabbed Sarah and pushed her inside

Dragnorr's carriage?" Hylrada asked.

"I don't know. I just had this overpowering feeling I'd seen him before, but he ducked down and the ripples blew everything out of focus right then." Gordon stopped rubbing his temples as the memory of that terrible migraine faded.

"Another spy for Dragnorr, I think," Sarah said. "Perhaps he ducked into the alley right before us and stole my Transporter?" Sarah raised her eyebrows.

"But, he didn't have a key." Gordon crossed his arms and leaned back on the station.

"Dragnorr used a key back at the ruins to open his Transporter. He may have some kind of universal key that can open others," Sarah suggested.

"And this spy of his had one too. It fits," Gordon agreed.

"Until we have more facts, our theories fit the available ones. But we must not close our minds to other possibilities," Hylrada said with a serious tone. "However, I am more concerned with the extreme state of temporal flux both of you experienced outside. It may have dire implications!"

"He's tampering with our world too much. Dragnorr can't play with time and space as if it were a game!" Gordon said angrily. He brushed his hands through his brown hair. "We've got to stop him."

"I am so afraid for Tom." Sarah turned to Gordon with an expression of deepest concern.

"Find Dragnorr, and you find the boy. I suggest you examine the data disc he dropped," Hylrada said simply.

"We've got to save the boy!" Sarah gasped as she gripped the disc tighter.

"Right, enough talking. We've got to rescue young Tom Walker first and then find out what Dragnorr's done to our world."

Gordon and Sarah ran over to the main console.

Sarah carefully placed the data disc into the slot.

They waited for the console to display the analysis of the disc and its contents, but the seconds ticked by with no activity.

All at once, every system and every console all around the Time Transporter grew active.

Gordon and Sarah stared in shock as myriads of lights flashed and messages scrolled in a blur across dozens of consoles.

Their eyes fixed on the Temporal Navigation display.

Chapter Twenty-Two

"We're jumping!" Gordon shouted.

They held on as the Transporter shuddered violently.

"Dragnorr tricked us!" Sarah cried as her body slammed back and forth with the shuddering of the Transporter's engines at full throttle.

"Gordon, you must override the controls," Hylrada said calmly above all the chaotic noise.

Gordon gripped the edge of the station and pulled himself carefully over to the Temporal Navigation station. He typed furiously and stabbed at various control buttons, and then he checked the settings.

"I can't budge the temporal settings -- they're locked in somehow." Gordon reached over to pull down a lever and checked the console again.

"No good. It's like he's sent some code to disable all the manual controls."

Sarah stumbled over to Spatial Navigation. She typed in a command and quickly turned a series of dials. She peered at the console.

"Controls are responding here -- somewhat."

Gordon raced over, falling against one station as the Transporter lurched and then running a few steps and being thrown against another. He reached out and collided with Sarah just as he reached her.

They disentangled themselves, and Gordon checked the console.

"Yes, there was some response, but it's gone back to the pre-defined settings from that disc!"

"Dragnorr is sending the Transporter into a set

of pre-defined coordinates. If you don't change them, you'll jump right into his waiting claws!" Hylrada warned.

"We know he's sending us straight into another trap!" Gordon said with a frustrated tone. "Tell us something that can help us."

"I am running an in-depth diagnostic on all the navigation systems as we speak," Hylrada said. "I have found where he has sent code to disable the manual controls. However, it seems the fine tuning controls on the spatial station are unaffected."

Gordon quickly took the dials to fine tune a landing and turned them hard over. He checked the console.

"We can't change the physical landing spot by much with just these controls." As he watched, the coordinates shifted over twenty kilometers from the pre-defined landing coordinates, but while he and Sarah continued to watch, the numbers slowly crept back to the original settings.

"They're still going back!" He twisted the dials hard over again.

"Gordon, the temporal coordinates indicate you are within sixty seconds of landing," Hylrada paused. "Wait for my command and turn the dials hard over one more time. This will put you further away from the spot he's expecting you -- and maybe far enough away his sensors might not notice you."

Gordon and Sarah looked quickly at each other.

"It's our only shot." Sarah's eyes opened wide as she shrugged.

"Right." Gordon placed both his hands on the dials and waited for Hylrada's command.

"Thirty seconds ... "

Gordon glanced at Sarah. She nodded her support.

"Twenty seconds ... "

Gordon readied himself.

"Twelve ... eleven ... NOW!"

Gordon pushed both dials hard over.

"Twenty kilometers off target," Gordon cried out.

"Five ... four ... "

"Eighteen kilometers off target."

"Three ... two ... "

"Fifteen kilometers."

"Zero."

But the shuddering of the Transporter continued unabated.

"Ten kilometers off target!" Gordon looked over at the communication console and Hylrada's visage. "Shall I put her over again?"

"You're too close in -- I'm afraid you would crash."

Hylrada looked down, and his eyes widened.

"Minus three seconds," Hylrada added.

"Five kilometers off target."

"Minus five ... "

Suddenly, Gordon and Sarah were flung across the room as the Transporter came to a screeching halt.

In the next seconds, alarms rang out as lights flicked on and off from every station and streams of escaping vapor hissed from several points in the ceiling and walls.

"We've lost integrity!" Sarah cried out as she

jumped up and ran over to the nearest jet of vapor. She typed rapidly. "I'm increasing shield strength to compensate for structural damage."

"Excellent!" Gordon shouted as he ran over to the main set of stations. "That wasn't the smoothest landing ever, now was it?"

"Worst one I've felt," Sarah shouted back.

"Yes, that Dragnorr probably meant us to have a hard landing -- damage the Transporter and make it harder for us to try and get away."

An alarm klaxon rang out with deafening volume.

"We've got a dangerous overload condition on the main power grid!" Gordon shouted as his expression froze with anxious concern.

"Gordon, I suggest you shut all systems down until you can effect repairs," Hylrada's voice said soothingly through Gordon's earpiece and all the speakers throughout the Transporter.

"Right, shutting down now."

"Gordon!" Sarah cried out. "If we shut everything down, how can we take off again?"

"If we don't shut down, we're going to blow up with a very large bang." Gordon locked eyes with Sarah.

"Guess we better prevent that first," Sarah said simply.

"Shutting down all systems," Gordon said as he typed commands at a furious pace first on one station and then a second right next to it. He then jumped a few steps aside to another and typed furiously again.

"Sarah! Help me!"

"I'm on it."

Sarah emulated his actions, typing shutdown commands at lightning speed.

Both of them shut down one station at a time and jumped to the next until they found themselves in front of the last station.

Sarah typed in the command and looked up.

"Done."

They both looked around at the silent consoles and stations all around the Transporter. Rawf barked happily.

"I don't like this," Gordon said.

"I've never seen all the systems shut down at once like this." Sarah walked over to the only live console -- the monitoring station. "Only sensors and shields are up."

"Any sign of Dragnorr?" Gordon stepped beside her and analyzed the sensor readings.

"No. No signs of any life within one kilometer of our present position."

Gordon leaned closer until his nose almost touched the glass of the console.

"Where are we?" He pulled back with an expression of shock. "I don't think we're on Earth any more."

Sarah's eyes widened as she peered at the readings. She gasped.

"No, you are very far away from your home world," Hylrada said.

"How far away?" Sarah asked.

"I'd say from glancing at your current coordinates that ... " Hylrada paused. "You are about halfway across the galaxy from Earth.

Hmmm, you are actually closer to my planet than yours at the moment."

"Just lovely!" Gordon said.

"What is this place?" Sarah turned a control.

Next to them, a console flickered to life. As they watched, the sensors sent a live feed.

Gordon and Sarah gasped as the alien world outside came into focus on the screen.

Chapter Twenty-Three

An exotic vista filled their eyes.

A pale, lavender sky with a single red sun first drew their interest. Then they noticed the huge clouds that sailed the sky in silent magnificence. Great mountainous shapes of whitish/reddish clouds were interspersed against the lavender sky.

A black lightning bolt streaked in a jagged line from one of the monstrous clouds down to the ground. A few seconds later, the rumbling of thunder rattled the Transporter.

Underneath the alien sky, the landscape was equally striking. The ground was multi-colored where the wind had whipped against it to reveal various shades of orange, brown, yellow and tan. A patchwork of countless barren hills each bordered by equally countless ravines stretched out in every direction as far as they could see.

And nowhere did there seem to be the first sign of life -- either vegetation or animal or insect.

"There's no life here?" Sarah asked.

"None register on sensors," Hylrada replied.

"What about Dragnorr?" Gordon grabbed two control dials and tuned them.

"No life for one kilometer in any direction," Hylrada added.

"There should be a ship. Or a Transporter. Or ... buildings, if Dragnorr is here." Sarah said.

"Two kilometers, no sign ... wait." Hylrada paused.

They waited with rising tension as Hylrada's pause seemed to stretch into hours.

"Sensors detect three structures on one of the hills just over two kilometers from your current position," Hylrada finally said.

"Yes, I see them," Gordon said. He pointed at the console, and Sarah stepped closer for a look.

"They seem rather primitive." Sarah peered at both the visual and analytical readings. "Reinforced concrete and steel for the walls. Hmmm, looks like a few window openings on the ground floor but nothing but wall all the way to the top. Metal domes on top of each -- some kind of steel alloy again. Wait ... "

Gordon focused on the domes.

"There is a tall and quite slender metal spire right on the very top of each dome." Gordon peered closer.

Suddenly, another bolt of black lightning streaked across the lavender sky between the monstrous clouds. The sky darkened as the black lightning bolt reached the other cloud, and both clouds glowed dark red where the ends of the lightning bolt entered or exited.

The black bolt glowed darker and fractured. Now, a second jagged line flashed out and downward. It struck one spire-tipped dome and almost instantly jumped to all three spires on top of each dome.

As they watched in awe, the domes began to glow with a surreal, black luminescence.

In the next second, a powerful rumbling shook everything inside the Transporter.

Rawf howled and tucked his four tails between his legs.

Gordon reached down and patted his head firmly to reassure him. "Don't worry, rog. It's all right."

Rawf wagged his tails excitedly for a second but immediately lowered his head in fear of the next round of rolling thunder.

"There are extraordinary power readings emanating from those structures," Gordon said. "Must be a lot of equipment inside them."

"Dragnorr's laboratory?" Hylrada suggested. "If it is, there may be extreme temporal fluctuations around those structures as well."

"Tampers with time a bit, does he?" Gordon asked in jest. He laughed mockingly.

"Like a mad scientist," Hylrada said.

"The maddest of them all!" Sarah said with a shake of head.

"What exactly is he doing, I wonder?" Gordon asked.

"No one knows." Hylrada sighed. "I have tried for a long time to try and figure out what he is up to. It's a mystery right now."

"We may find out -- when we get inside." Sarah looked at Gordon.

He smiled and shook his head. Gordon turned his attention to another console.

"Where did we land, by the way?" Gordon peered excitedly at the sensor logs. "Are we on top of one of these hillocks and in plain sensor view?"

"No, you have landed deep inside one of the maze of ravines that crisscross all these thousands of bare hills," Hylrada replied.

"Good -- they may not have seen us yet."

"Where did our original coordinates have us landing?" Sarah twirled a few dials and typed a command. "We should have landed ... right in the middle of a courtyard in front of the first two domed structures. They stand side by side with this courtyard in front. Directly behind them is the largest domed structure."

"Instead, we are just over two kilometers east." Gordon smiled proudly.

"All three are connected by huge, walled passageways," Hylrada told them after he reviewed the visuals from the Transporter.

"Try a quick sensor scan," Gordon suggested.

"Won't they detect that?" Sarah asked.

"Do it fast, a quick sweep," Gordon urged.

Sarah's fingers danced over the controls a moment.

They both peered at the console.

"Nothing!" they said together.

"Sensors can't penetrate the buildings." Hylrada said thoughtfully. "That could be a problem when you get inside."

"But maybe their sensors won't be able to detect us once we're inside." Gordon looked at Sarah hopefully.

"Should we wait before we try?" Sarah's expression grew serious.

"No, we take off right away. The longer we don't show up, the wider Dragnorr may extend his sensor sweeps around the area. He's still expecting us to land at our original landing spot per the settings on the disc."

"I concur," Hylrada said. "I have calculated a

path that will allow you both to keep inside the ravines up to the edge of Dragnorr's hill. You will be out of sight the entire way and underneath any stray sensor sweep."

"I have one Stunner left." Gordon picked up a Time Rod. "And one of these from the Anon."

"Take both. The Time Rod may be useful."

"I have my handheld sensor. It should help until we get inside." Sarah held it up.

"Is the atmosphere breathable for humans?" Gordon asked.

"Yes, the atmosphere is safe for humans to breathe. I've just reviewed the sensor readings on it. However, it is quite cold outside," Hylrada said.

Gordon put on his full coat. He switched off the Time Rod and put it inside his coat pocket, hidden out of sight. He placed the Stunner in its holster. He looked at Sarah.

She buttoned her floor-length coat and wrapped a long scarf around her neck. She smiled to indicate she was ready.

Gordon raised his key, and the door opened to reveal the exotic beauty of this otherworld.

Gordon and Sarah rushed through and started running down the ravine toward Dragnorr's bunker with the rog right beside them.

They had taken two full steps when both Gordon and Sarah stopped instantly and covered their faces with both their hands as they cried out.

Rawf sneezed three times in rapid succession.

"Is there danger?" Hylrada's voice echoed in their earpieces.

"It smells like a giant fart!" Gordon gagged. He

211

used his fingers to pinch his nose against the overwhelming stench.

"Can you be more specific -- what exactly smells like a giant fart?"

"Everything!" Gordon and Sarah shouted together.

Sarah coughed continuously.

"Oh yes, well, I just reviewed my analysis in more detail. There is a slightly elevated concentration of sulphur and other odds and ends in the atmosphere. I imagine it may have a *distinct* odor compared to Earth." Hylrada said in a calm, matter-of-fact tone.

"I can't breathe!" Gordon shouted.

"Of course you can -- it has the right amount of all the essential elements required for humans. It just ... "

"Stinks like a giant fart!"

Gordon looked over at Sarah. "Shall we run for it?"

Sarah wavered unsteadily. "I feel faint."

"I feel like I'm going to vomit." Gordon pinched his nose tighter.

"You'd best hurry. Perhaps the air inside the building is *conditioned* ... "

Gordon and Sarah broke out in a full run with that hopeful thought. As they sprinted through the ravine for all they were worth, they breathed solely through their mouths.

A short time later, after crisscrossing the maze of ravines, they found themselves at the base of the domed structures sitting on the hill. They had made their way by a combination of Hylrada's directions

212

and by using Sarah's scanner.

Another bolt of black lightning flashed through the air followed almost immediately by the rumbling of thunder.

"Well, here we go."

Gordon started climbing with Sarah and Rawf right behind. Hylrada's directions now led them up toward a side entrance, which they hoped was not well guarded.

"Hold on!" Sarah stared at her handheld as she tapped on the controls.

"What is it?" Gordon whispered.

"I'm reading something just around the corner. It's in another ravine farther up the base of this hill ... " Sarah looked up with a shocked expression. "It's our missing Time Transporter!"

"What?"

They sprinted to the ravine. Sarah led the way, keeping her eye on her handheld as it directed them to the source of its sensor readings. A few minutes later, she pulled up the necklace from around her neck and held up her Transporter key.

The outline of a door shimmered in the air and grew solid an instant later.

Gordon and Sarah exchanged thoroughly surprised glances.

They walked quickly inside with Rawf, and the door shut behind them.

Gordon looked around with his mouth hanging open in shock.

"Everything seems to be here." Sarah walked around examining shelves and consoles with a keen eye for detail.

213

"How did it get here?" Gordon asked.

"A good question," Hylrada said in their earpieces.

"Whoever stole it must be inside Dragnorr's bunkers above us," Sarah declared.

"Yes ... but if they worked for Dragnorr, or had stolen it for him, why land outside his laboratory? If they were expected by Dragnorr, or if they were an ally or friend of Dragnorr, they should have landed inside. Why land outside here in a ravine ... as if to hide their landing?" Hylrada asked.

"They're not an ally then. And they're not expected." Gordon snapped his fingers. "And so, they land just outside in one of the ravines out of sight ... and probably undetected by Dragnorr!"

"They obviously wanted the landing to be undetected from Dragnorr. And that means ... what?" Hylrada paused again.

"The mystery gets deeper and deeper." Sarah's eyes widened with curiosity.

"Were there any footsteps outside?" Hylrada asked.

"The ground is hard like rock everywhere -- no dust, no dirt. No footprints are possible." Gordon began pacing around as he thought intensely of the implications.

"And nothing is missing inside?"

"Everything is just as I left it," Sarah replied.

"So, they steal it and jump to the very spot where Dragnorr tricked us into landing?" Gordon thought out loud.

"Near the very time you are expected ... " Hylrada added.

"Scary," Sarah said with a tone of grave concern.

"And, it seems they must have made a secretive entrance into the bunkers at precisely the spot we determined would make the best place to enter undetected." Hylrada paused with thought.

"Scarier and scarier." Sarah frowned with concern.

"Then, whoever stole our Transporter may be an enemy of Dragnorr too."

"And a potential ally for us?" Sarah added with hope.

"I'm not sure we can extrapolate that with such limited facts," Hylrada said.

"We'll have to keep an eye out for this mysterious person," Gordon said with a cautious tone.

"And we already have enough to deal with in Dragnorr and his minions." Sarah crossed her arms firmly.

Gordon took a deep breath and spoke. "Let's make our entry as quickly and quietly as possible now and rescue Tom. If necessary, we can use this Transporter and jump back for the other later. Since we have this unknown entity added to the mix, I think it best to go as stealthily as possible from here."

Sarah nodded.

"Better leave Rawf inside the Transporter then," Hylrada suggested.

"Yes, he might draw attention once inside," Sarah said.

"Agreed," Gordon said. "I thought he might help

us fight off the Shadows if it came down to a battle, but he does tend to bark at the most inopportune times."

"Be careful, my friends," Hylrada said with concern. "There's something or someone inside those bunkers that we don't fully understand yet. Their mysterious presence adds an unknown risk to your venture."

"Very much so," Gordon said. "I'm not sure who to be more concerned with right now -- Dragnorr or this *other* person ... "

Chapter Twenty-Four

As Gordon and Sarah climbed up toward the nearest window opening on the east wall, the entire wall and even the sky above shimmered as if suddenly fluid.

Gordon froze.

"Did you see that?" Sarah whispered urgently.

But as suddenly as it occurred, everything became stable and solid.

Gordon felt his stomach cramp with pain.

"Another temporal fluctuation?" Hylrada whispered in their earpieces.

"A brief one," Gordon whispered.

Sarah placed her hand on Gordon's arm and squeezed him reassuringly.

Gordon continued up until he was just below the opening.

There was no glass and no grate within the opening -- he looked inside and saw a large room.

Gordon swung his leg over and hopped inside. He reached out and helped Sarah through. They turned and surveyed the room.

It was empty -- and it was huge.

The gray walls were smooth and devoid of anything as they stretched all around the large room. The ceiling was high above them.

Gordon looked back at the opening. On the ledge, he noticed the scuff marks where he and Sarah had entered.

He also saw a third pair of scuff marks where the mysterious other had entered before them.

Gordon looked closer.

Suddenly, a curtain of flowing light appeared between him and the opening. It looked remarkably similar to the curtain of flowing light he and Sarah had stepped through in the alley.

He hesitated.

And stepped through.

He felt disoriented -- just like before. But this time, the dizziness faded quickly.

Gordon examined the scuff marks.

"I think the mysterious other is human." Gordon pointed at the ledge. "Two scuff marks -- two shoes on the ledge. Just like ours beside it."

Gordon looked around the large room.

He focused on a door near the far end.

"That seems to be the only door," Sarah said simply.

"Ah Sarah, you have a way with the obvious."

Gordon took off at a run, with Sarah following close behind.

When they reached the middle of the room, the air above them began to glow.

Gordon and Sarah paused and looked upward.

A strange mist began to expand in the air and then to glow. In the next instant, the mist took shape and became a huge, flowing curtain of glowing light.

Gordon and Sarah gasped. They turned and backed away, staring up at it.

Muffled voices came out of the wavering curtain of glowing light. And suddenly, vague images became barely discernable.

"What is it?" Sarah whispered fearfully.

"What are you seeing?" Hylrada asked.

218

Gordon quickly described it as they watched in fascination.

"Time communication," Hylrada said.

"How do you know?" Gordon whispered.

"I recognize it. I use one to view into the ether and focus on temporal settings within a specific spatial focus. Although the one I use is quite small, it still allows me to view other worlds through time -- and to view any time period in history."

"Wow, Dragnorr has one on a very, big scale."

As they watched, the shapes took form.

"Romans!" Sarah whispered aloud. "Legions of Roman soldiers and ... I see temples and the buildings of an ancient city behind them."

"You are viewing part of Earth's history," Hylrada said. "Dragnorr has been most interested in Earth's history lately."

"I don't like it," Gordon said with anger.

"Let's get on." Sarah began running for the door.

Gordon raced beside her. They made it to the door and cautiously looked out.

The room outside was several times larger than the one they were inside. The walls again were bare and devoid of anything. And high, high above, the curve of the great dome formed the ceiling of this huge room.

They glanced down. Their view was fantastic. They were several stories above floor level of the vast room before them. Gordon and Sarah stood on a narrow ledge -- perhaps some kind of walkway used by maintenance staff -- that ran the length of the great room and ended up at a huge open doorway at the rear. The walkway disappeared around the edge of the rear opening and most likely continued around the wall into the next room beyond.

But the wall opposite them had no such walkway.

They surveyed the vast room below them.

Everywhere they looked, they saw row upon row of stations with Anons sitting before them, each staring resolutely forward at a small curtain of glowing mist.

"They're all observing portals of Time!" Sarah whispered in surprise.

"There must be thousands of Anon down there." Gordon glanced around the huge room.

The impression was a vast call center with all the workers sitting diligently at their stations waiting to answer a phone call for help.

But each individual here was exactly alike. Each Anon was dressed in a long, flowing black robe with matching black hood. They all sat frozen, each staring at the shimmering curtain of light before them. But they had no eyes on their smooth, featureless face of silver skin crisscrossed with black lines.

"They don't move much, do they? Kind of odd," Gordon said.

"How do they see, I wonder?" Sarah raised her eyebrows in a quandary.

"I think the crisscrossing black lines provide all their sensory input -- smell, hearing, sight," Gordon put his hand on his chin as if in thought.

"They give me the creeps -- not having a face and all." Sarah shivered.

"Not as bad as the Shadows, I think." Gordon shrugged.

Gordon felt a slight dizziness that heralded the return of his vertigo. The great room before him shivered and then began to flow as if liquid. As he stared, it seemed the whole room fluttered like a huge curtain in a wind.

He groaned as his stomach cramped painfully. He turned away as the room danced harder.

And at the corner of his vision in the distance, he caught the briefest glimpse of a man running around a corner out of sight.

"I saw him."

"What?" Sarah turned to follow his stare. "I don't see anything."

"He's gone now, but I saw a man running round that far corner."

"It must have been our mysterious 'other.'" Sarah searched Gordon's eyes.

"Why is he here?" Gordon wondered out loud.

They turned back to the rows upon rows of silent, watching Anon.

"And what are they looking for?" Gordon brushed his hands through his brown hair. "Thousands of them peering into portals of time -- probably each observing a different part of history."

"And are they observing the timeline of a single world -- or many worlds?" Hylrada's whisper echoed in both their earpieces.

"Come on -- we better get going." Gordon started forward.

"Where are we going?" Sarah asked.

"Toward the biggest dome." Gordon pointed

toward the far end of the vast room. "And that's where our mystery guest headed as well."

They made their way along the walkway. This narrow path hugged the wall three stories above the main floor of the great room below. They pressed themselves against the wall in an effort to make themselves as unobtrusive as possible.

"What about your hand-held? Is it working in here?" Gordon whispered over his shoulder.

Sarah held it up and typed a few commands. She frowned a moment, adjusted two dials and typed more. With a sigh, she dropped her arm back down to her side with the hand-held still in her grasp and hurried forward to catch Gordon.

"Nothing. It's like there's some kind of fog -- electronic fog -- that prevents any readings." Sarah looked behind, the first time she had thought to check their backs.

In the far distance, she saw the doorway where they had entered the great room from the first room.

As she stared, she noticed movement -- as if someone was about to come out onto the walkway behind them.

"Someone's coming!" Sarah whispered urgently.

Gordon glanced back and saw two Anon just reaching the doorway.

"Run!"

They broke into a full run.

A few seconds later they rounded the same corner where Gordon had caught the glimpse of the mystery person.

Gordon paused and chanced a look back.

The walkway was empty.

"Seems they didn't come out," Gordon said.

"You don't see them on the walkway?"

"No, they must have changed their mind."

"Let's hurry," Sarah said, her voice rushed with emotion. "I don't want to stay in this place any longer than we have to."

They found themselves inside some kind of intermediary room between the two domed buildings. This room was tiny compared to the great room behind them, and close above them was a flat ceiling. Below them were two more identical walkways on the first two levels.

"There must have been two more walkways directly below us back in the great room," Gordon observed.

"Strange, the opposite wall was completely featureless -- no walkways or doorways or anything." Sarah shook her head.

They both noticed the closed door straight ahead of them.

"I guess we've got to enter through that." Gordon nodded toward it.

"The other person must have entered that way too."

"You're right, Sarah." Gordon glanced around.

There were no other doors except the one they entered and the one before them.

"I imagine the two walkways below us lead to a door as well."

They moved forward cautiously.

Gordon placed his hand upon the door and pushed it forward just enough so he could see inside. He placed his cheek against the coolness of the door and looked.

There was a room down below even larger than the one they'd left. And again, there were almost endless rows of Anon sitting frozen as they stared at small curtains of rippling light.

Unlike the previous great room, there was a flat ceiling above them. But both Gordon and Sarah knew that above that ceiling somewhere was the largest steel dome.

Gordon looked to his left.

The walkway led to another door and room beyond.

He pushed the door open enough so he and Sarah could slip inside.

He looked back to his right and saw another closed door.

"Which way now?" Sarah whispered.

"I think there is a room above the ceiling. There's nothing but Anon out there, so there must be a way up to the next level through one of these doors." Gordon looked left and then right.

"Let's try the right one," Sarah suggested.

"Let's go."

They hurried to the closed door, and Gordon again slowly opened it as he peeked through the crack.

Everything was cloaked in darkness.

"Not good," Gordon whispered.

"I've got a small torch." Sarah reached inside her coat and switched it on. She shined the beam inside.

It was a small room with two doors against the far wall. But as she shone the beam around, they spotted a narrow stairwell leading upward.

224

"That way."

Gordon led the way as he stepped quickly upward.

They had climbed perhaps two stories when they came to a closed door.

Gordon pulled out his Stunner and placed his shoulder against the door. He looked at Sarah.

"Switch off your torch."

She nodded.

He pushed the door open and stepped inside.

Complete darkness greeted them.

Sarah followed him inside.

A cool dampness caressed their faces as if a breeze blew inside this darkened room. Above them, they sensed rather than saw the curved inner surface of the dome rising high above them.

Gordon glanced up.

The darkness seemed to move high above them, like a black curtain rippling slowly on a night wind.

The door closed behind them.

Suddenly, a blaze of red lights shone upon them from a dozen spots around them.

Gordon and Sarah raised their hands to their eyes in quick reaction.

Gordon felt his heart freeze.

"Welcome, Gordon Smith and Sarah Nightingale. We've been expecting you."

Dragnorr clicked his mandibles in delight while a dozen Anon stood on either side of him holding red torches in their hands.

"Well, there's goes our surprise rescue," Gordon said with a shrug.

Chapter Twenty-Five

Dragnorr led them farther inside as the Anon kept watch on Gordon and Sarah.

They had quickly removed his Stunner and the Time Rod inside his inner coat pocket. They had also taken Sarah's hand-held and her torch.

A few moments later, Dragnorr led them up another set of stairs until they entered a poorly lit room filled with consoles and electronics. In every direction, small lights twinkled like stars on all the rows of equipment.

"This is the heart of my laboratory." Dragnorr spread his arms.

Gordon and Sarah walked inside and stood before the black creature.

"What have you done with young Tom?" Gordon asked firmly.

"The boy?" Dragnorr hissed with surprise. "He is nothing, merely the bait to motivate you into quick action and to use the disc I dropped before you examined it too closely."

"But we didn't land where you expected us?" Gordon smiled.

"You are full of surprises, Gordon." Dragnorr raised himself to his full height of nine feet.

"How do you two do it?" Dragnorr hissed. "You manage to escape every trap I set for you. Somehow you evade my Shadows, no matter how many I send. You even outsmart my Anon. How do you do it?"

"We're smart *and* good looking." Gordon smiled and turned to Sarah.

He winked mischievously at her.

Sarah laughed and winked back.

"You'll find no humor here in my lair," Dragnorr growled. "I have you at last."

He leaned over until his black face was right before Gordon's face.

"You won't escape me now."

"Well, we just arrived, haven't we? Give us a few moments -- I'm sure one of us will come up with something." Gordon chuckled.

"You two have been a thorn in my side for too long." Dragnorr hissed as he straightened.

"Are we?" Gordon scratched the side of his head.

"Ever since my Anon discovered your 'Folkestone Project', yes!"

Gordon and Sarah exchanged a quick glance.

"Right." Gordon put his hands deep in his coat pockets. "And how was it you discovered our little project again? I assume one of your Anon here found it viewing their portals into Earth's timeline, perhaps?"

"Yes, Gordon Smith. There's really no need for me to hide anything from either of you now. In a few moments, I will have my Anon send each of you on a one-way trip into time -- with no way back!" Dragnorr laughed hysterically.

"That part doesn't sound like much fun." Gordon glanced around the room filled with the twinkling lights and the vast number of computers.

"You don't remember the others, do you?" Dragnorr asked as he finally stopped laughing.

"Others?" Sarah said with surprise.

"Oh yes, there were seven of you originally."

Gordon felt surprised as well.

"Where are they now?" Sarah asked in a defensive tone.

"Oh, I disposed of them one way or another. Some are lost in time -- with no way back. Others are ... shall we say, no longer in existence in any time."

"Why?" Gordon asked firmly. "Why all this? Why do you want to monitor our world's timeline?"

"Power. Control. Rulership."

"Everyone wants to rule the world," Sarah said tiredly.

"Ruling a single world -- that's for amateurs!" Dragnorr hissed.

"Ah, so what is it you *really* want to do?"

"I want to control Earth. And not just your world, but all the others in this part of the galaxy. I want to control far more than a single age! For if I control the timeline, I have control over everything and everyone in every era!" Dragnorr clicked his mandibles twice.

"Your Anon are watching Earth's history?" Sarah asked.

"Yes, many thousands of Anon sit and monitor the timeline of Earth. They search for any disturbances in the ether -- searching for tell-tale signs of time travel." Dragnorr began pacing around them.

"And ... "

"And, when we find evidence of time travel -- we investigate."

"Ah, I see. If someone on Earth begins to

experiment with time travel, you discover it and then stop it."

"Exactly! If I am the only creature with the ability to travel through time, that means I can control everything about your world." Dragnorr raised his long arms until his talons pointed to the darkness above. "I can go back to any point in Earth's history and make a subtle tweak and change history according to my desire. If some fool begins to discover time travel, I send my Anon back and prevent it!"

"How?" Sarah asked. "How can you prevent it, if they're already on the verge of it?"

"Perhaps I send my Anon back a few years prior to the experiments and change something in the scientist's past?"

"Like a car accident? Kill him before he even begins his experiments!" Sarah said with shock.

"Yesssss," Dragnorr hissed. "There are other methods we use. On some worlds, we tinker with the political climate so that time travel is feared so badly they will outlaw such experiments!"

Gordon froze as he heard Hylrada gasp inside his earpiece.

"Whenever any world we monitor gets too close, I calculate what the simplest, most effective change is necessary in order to back it out or prevent it from happening! It's almost too easy sometimes."

Dragnorr laughed as he again began pacing around the room.

"And yet, you feared our team from Folkestone?" Gordon countered.

"Yes!"

Dragnorr stopped right before Gordon and Sarah.

"You don't remember any of it, do you?" Dragnorr asked.

"Afraid not." Gordon shrugged as he scratched the side of his head.

"Yes, your Folkestone was the first project of its kind in the entire timeline of Earth."

"Someone suspected you were out here tampering with us, didn't they?" Sarah smiled confidently.

"Yes! The leaders of your little group had come to the conclusion that someone was stepping in and preventing anyone from ever succeeding in developing time travel." Dragnorr crossed his long, black arms. "Yes, somehow they deduced from a careful analysis of all the failed experiments before them. I grew careless at my seemingly endless success in pushing back your feeble efforts to join me."

"A long trail of tampering that was finally recognized," Gordon said as if remembering someone else saying the same thing.

"Yes."

"And, our project was conducted with that knowledge. So, all our initial attempts were conducted in such a way so as to avoid detection. And, once we succeeded ... " Gordon paused as the memories came flooding back.

"Once we succeeded, we formed a team to travel into the ether and seek out and stop those that were tampering with our timeline," Sarah finished for him.

"Yes, you came here searching for me -- to destroy me and my power!"

"You're insane, Dragnorr," Sarah said. "You don't just want to control our world -- you want to control everything! Our past, our present, our future! You manipulate us like puppets -- for what?"

"Power ... greed ... to fulfill any of my wildest desires! It is so exhilarating to wield such power. Just think of it -- I can change anything at a whim!"

"You're mad with power, completely insane! You can't control everyone and everything!" Sarah cried.

Dragnorr laughed.

The black creature turned to Gordon.

"And you?"

"You're totally bonkers, Dragnorr. Way beyond professional help, in my opinion."

Dragnorr laughed hysterically.

"And, what did you do when you found out about Folkestone?" Sarah asked.

"Oh, I had to calculate my attack very carefully for you." Dragnorr clicked his mandibles. "Yes, I needed to cover my trail -- undo some of my past tampering or make those changes more subtle. Then, I had to prevent some of the key members of Folkestone from ever forming that project -- whether by unfortunate accidents or any other modification."

"And *us*?" Gordon shouted. "What did you do to Sarah and me? We don't exist in Earth's timeline any longer -- we don't exist any longer!"

"I know."

231

"Did you prevent us from being born?" Gordon asked with firmness.

"That was the ultimate effect, but of course, my changes to the timeline were not that simple. Actually, I changed your family history for several generations!"

"You monster!" Sarah shouted.

"You must understand -- I had to put a lot of thought into getting rid of you two. Don't you see?"

"Of course," Gordon paused as his thoughts coalesced. "We can travel through time like you."

"Yes. I go back and forth in time and change things according to my desire. But, if I made only a simple change to attack either of you, well, you could possibly travel back in time and ... "

"Right!" Sarah said with sudden discernment. "We were the first ones to fight you in your own element and on your own level."

"Yes, once we discovered you, we could possibly make a change and perhaps somehow undo some of what you've done. Or, get rid of you one way or another using our ability to travel through time." Gordon nodded.

"So, if I made too simple an alteration to change your past, you could possibly travel back in tine and undo it. I had to carefully plan my attacks on both of you -- just as I had to eradicate the Folkestone Project and its leaders."

"Bonkers," Gordon repeated.

"But, you two did not disappear when I changed your past. Before, when I changed things in order to prevent a person's being born, my target simply disappeared -- they no longer existed, period."

"But, not us ... " Gordon said, remembering Hylrada's theories.

"Right, not you two. When I made my change, you were living among the ether between time and space. I had not taken that into account. All the others were living in normal space/time when I made my change."

"So, we escaped."

"Yes, with help from that furry meddler Hylrada! Without his interference, I would have destroyed you long ago."

Gordon heard Hylrada's quick intake of breath.

"My equipment can detect time travel but not communication through the ether. Hylrada has slowly been building a network of others who have perfected such communication. And more, his growing network is beginning to experiment with traveling through time. But so far, my Anon have detected and undone all their attempts. But they are growing more adept -- like Folkestone."

"Good old Hylrada!" Sarah said proudly.

"I need to pinpoint the exact point in space/time where Hylrada exists so I can deal with him once and for all!"

Gordon raised his eyebrows in surprise as he tugged on the ear with his ear-piece.

"You heard that?" Gordon whispered.

"Yes. If he ever finds my exact temporal location, he'll come and change something to destroy me or my work," Hylrada whispered as low as possible.

"After I disposed of the other five from your team, I tried to erase both of you by removing you from your timeline. You two are the best. You two are worthy enemies of me, Dragnorr. Now, I must remove of you once and for all before you grow too adept, too dangerous." Dragnorr growled.

"So, our project was to find you and stop you." Gordon nodded as more memories came into focus.

"And you've failed. Today, I shall get rid of you both. And very soon now, I will find Hylrada and get rid of him as well!"

"And then?" Gordon asked.

"And then, I shall rule worlds. And not just worlds, but *all time* as well!"

Chapter Twenty-Six

Without warning, the darkened room shimmered and grew fluid all around them.

Gordon felt a sudden overwhelming sense of déjà vu again. He quickly turned and surveyed the darkened room filled with twinkling lights. As he looked, the feeling that he'd been here before turned into absolute certainty.

And now the entire room and everything in it danced and shimmered crazily. Gordon's knees buckled as he started to collapse. It felt as if he were falling into the shimmering fluid of time all around ...

Two of the Anon grabbed him by either arm.

"What is going on?" Dragnorr shouted angrily. "Don't just stand there -- check the readings! Find out what that was!"

Gordon wavered unsteadily as the dizziness passed.

"Are you all right?" Sarah whispered to him.

"I got that strange feeling again ... like everything around me is unstable ... or fluid." Gordon rubbed his eyes.

Three Anon ran over and stood before a separate computer station. After a few moments analysis, one of them spoke.

"There was a disturbance in the ether around us!"

"At this very moment?" Dragnorr shouted.

"Yes, sir. Something or someone is here and causing ... "

Gordon and Sarah glanced quickly at each other.

Dragnorr turned and grabbed Gordon and lifted him up until his face pressed against the black shininess of his own.

"What have you done, Gordon Smith?"

"I haven't done anything -- that I know of."

"Only a time traveler can disturb the ether like that!"

"Well, I guess there must be somebody else here who can travel through time, because I've been right here the entire time ... time, in a manner of speaking."

"Silence!"

In the low light of the vast computer room, the myriads of twinkling lights changed all at once. Where before they had twinkled rapidly like the stars in heaven, now the rapid flickering patterns slowed.

Dragnorr, Gordon and the others all looked around in surprise.

And one by one, the twinkling lights began to go out.

"What's happening now?" Dragnorr shouted.

As the three Anon typed commands at their stations, sparks and explosions erupted at the far end of the room. Smoke rose rapidly as the twinkling patterns of lights grew more unstable, and dozens began to flash out completely every second.

"Sabotage!" Dragnorr shouted. "Sound the alarms! Order all Anon to begin a search for other infiltrators!"

Most of the Anon around them ran in various directions as red lights flashed and alarms sounded.

Dragnorr put Gordon down and nodded at him

and Sarah.

Four Anon grabbed Gordon and Sarah by their arms and held them fast.

"Bring them. It's time to dispose of them once and for all."

Dragnorr marched forward with the others behind him.

They reached the far end of the room and walked through the shower of sparks while several computers continued to smoke and sputter.

The small room was dominated by a single portal station with a large chair.

"This is your personal Time Portal for viewing time, eh?" Gordon asked.

"Yes, this is my inner sanctum." Dragnorr walked over to a closed curtain. He pushed it open.

"Tom!" Sarah cried out.

"Miss Sarah!" Tom cried joyfully.

Young Tom Walker stood with his wrists shackled to the wall.

"Are you all right, Tom?" Gordon asked.

Tom gasped.

As Tom looked from Sarah to Gordon, his expression changed from joy to pure shock.

"It's you, Mr. Smith!" Tom cried in surprise.

"Of course! I'm usually somewhere close by when there's trouble." Gordon chuckled.

"But how ... " Tom looked over his shoulder and back at Gordon.

Gordon suddenly felt dizzy again. The Anon gripped him tighter as he swayed.

As he looked at Tom, the boy and the air around him shimmered as if fluid.

"Enough of the pleasantries -- it's time to get rid of you both." Dragnorr walked back to his station and used his giant talons to type.

"Anon, put their weapons and tools here."

As quickly as it happened, everything became solid again around Tom again.

Gordon stared at the boy.

Tom nodded and smiled again as he wiggled his fingers.

It seemed to Gordon as if Tom were trying to send him a secret message without speaking any words, but he didn't quite get it.

An Anon placed Gordon's Stunner and the Time Rod on the desk beside Dragnorr. He reached in his black robe and pulled out Sarah's torch and her hand-held sensor and placed them there as well.

"Take the woman into the Time Tunnel!"

"No!"

Sarah began struggling against the two Anon holding her.

Gordon also fought against the vise-like grips of the two Anon who held him, but they were stronger than they looked. No matter how hard he struggled or kicked or lashed out, they held him fast.

Slowly, they took the still struggling Sarah toward a small set of steps that led to an armored door.

"Sarah!" Gordon cried out.

"Gordon! Help me!"

Gordon felt his heart pounding like a jackhammer as he tried to break free.

And as he watched them open the door and take her inside, he felt his heart breaking in two.

"What are you going to do to her?" Gordon demanded angrily.

"What my Anon have tried and failed. They will strap her into a chair, and then I will issue a command to start up the Time Tunnel. I will set the randomizer to maximum setting and then send her back into the past -- a point in the timeline unknown even to me. For as soon as she is sent back, the randomizer will change the setting with no way for any of us to go back and find her!"

"You monster!" Gordon shouted.

"And you will be next. I will send you somewhere into the primitive past. You will have no technology to help you there -- neither of you. You will both live out your pitiful existence unable to get back at me or to find each other. You will each grow old and die."

Gordon felt a sudden panic grip his heart. He realized how terrible it would be to never see Sarah again -- never hear her voice, her laughter.

He would live out his life without her -- alone. And die an old man lost in time.

"I see by your expression that you realize how permanent my solution will be. I will finally be rid of you both! And more, I will hurt you beyond killing you."

"What do you mean?" Gordon asked as if in a daze.

"You will be utterly alone without her, Gordon Smith -- even your dreams will be filled with a melancholy that will haunt your every waking moment. You will begin to feel like an orphan -- that devastating loneliness of having never been loved and the awful dread that you never will ... "

Dragnorr laughed with a maniacal glow in his red eyes. The twin pincers at the tip of his mandibles clicked in rapid-fire succession.

"If I can't kill you, at least I can crush your heart so that life won't be worth living any more!" Dragnorr hissed sadistically.

Gordon shut his eyes against the heart-rending possibility.

"She is strapped in the chair, Dragnorr." The Anon's low voice emanated from a speaker on Dragnorr's console.

"Good -- stand aside while I enable the Time Tunnel."

Gordon opened his eyes and watched Dragnorr type the final command. Dragnorr raised his head, and his glowing red eyes stared right through Gordon.

"I will now press the button to send her away from you forever."

Sarah screamed, and the ear-piercing wail sent chills through Gordon's body.

"No!" Gordon yelled out.

He looked from one Anon grasping his arm to the other. Both stared sightlessly right at Dragnorr as he prepared to hit the final button.

Gordon suddenly dropped to his knees and pulled both Anon down with him in a heap.

He kicked out with his legs and caught the Anon on his right with a good blow to his abdomen. The Anon fell to the side, gasping for air and releasing his arm, although the other held on tight.

Gordon struck out with his right fist as the Anon

struck at him.

They rolled on the ground struggling and exchanging blows.

"Control him!" Dragnorr hissed angrily.

He finally managed to wrench his arm free and jumped up.

Before him, the Anon rose up to face him.

"Get away from me!" Gordon shouted.

Dragnorr's talon clicked the button.

"She is gone!" he hissed.

"No!"

Gordon glanced behind and saw the other Anon rising to join the fray. He clenched his fists and readied himself.

He looked back at the other Anon just as he attacked.

Suddenly, a Stunner blast sent the Anon hard to the ground.

"*What?*" Gordon asked.

Tom Walker stood free with the Stunner in his hand. He turned quickly, fired two blasts and felled the other Anon.

"Anon in the Time Tunnel room, come here! Gordon is free!" Dragnorr shouted.

But only silence answered.

The black monster lurched upward with his two talons raised at him in a threatening gesture. "I will have to deal with you myself, it seems!"

Tom fired the Stunner at point blank range.

Dragnorr bent over and fell across the computer station and console.

"Here, Mr. Smith!"

Tom threw the Time Rod at him.

Gordon's eyes widened with surprise as the staff twirled through the air in a high arc towards him.

Dragnorr lashed out with his leg to strike Tom and sent him flying.

The Stunner flew out of Tom's grasp and slithered against the far wall.

The huge monster leaped at Gordon with talons raised to slash him open.

Gordon caught the Time Rod and flicked the switch.

He jumped to the side just as Dragnorr reached him.

A talon ripped a long gash into his coat as he fell just out of the monster's reach.

Gordon rolled several times and jumped quickly up with the active Time Rod pointed at Dragnorr. Sparks and tiny bolts of electricity shot out of it as he held it steady.

"Don't come any closer!" Gordon warned.

"You can't do it, Gordon. If you shoot me into time, how will you ever hope to undo what I've done to you and your precious Sarah? You'll never figure it out by yourself!"

Gordon hesitated.

Dragnorr leaped for Gordon, his talons aimed at Gordon's throat.

Gordon pressed the contact. A shower of sparks erupted, and a wave of electric bolts shot out.

Dragnorr screamed as he seemed to stop in mid-air.

As Gordon stared, the black creature's body sparkled and shimmered.

In the next moment, Dragnorr disappeared.

242

Gordon switched off the Time Rod and ran over to Tom.

"Mr. Smith, is he gone?"

Gordon quickly checked the lad over.

"Nothing seems to be broken, Tom. You're just going to have some painful bruises."

"Miss Sarah!" Tom shouted.

Gordon jumped up.

He ran over and grabbed his Stunner while placing the Time Rod back in his inner coat pocket.

"Grab Sarah's hand-held sensor and her torch, Tom!"

He raced up to the heavy steel door and opened it. Gordon raced inside.

He stopped and stared at the empty chair in the middle of the darkened room.

"No!" he cried.

He ran up to the chair and grabbed at it, as if somehow he could bring her back.

"No ... no ... no!" he kept repeating as his worst fears came true.

"Look!" Tom pointed.

He turned and saw two Anon lying on the floor, unconscious.

"What?" He raced over and checked them.

Both were stunned.

"Who could have done that?" Gordon bent over them while his mind worked at light speed.

"Who put them out?" Tom asked.

"I don't know!" Gordon jumped up and did a quick survey of the room.

There seemed to be only one way into this room, and that was through the door by which

243

they'd just entered.

"What about the secret door?" Tom asked.

"What secret door?" Gordon frowned in shock at the boy's words. "How would you know about a secret door into this place?"

Suddenly, a string of explosions shook the entire building down to its very foundation.

"We'd better get out of here now. The whole place is going to explode in a few minutes," Tom said matter-of-factly.

Gordon grasped Tom by his shoulders as he leaned down and looked deeply into Tom's eyes.

"Where did learn all this, Tom?"

"You told me!"

Gordon felt his heart pounding so hard and so fast it felt like it would leap out of his chest. He wavered a moment as everything became fluid and shimmered in a surreal wave.

Everything swirled around him as if in a dream.

"Gordon ... " Hylrada's voice sounded as if it were a million miles away.

Gordon tugged at his earpiece as a strange buzzing grew louder and louder.

Gordon's vision blurred. A fog filled the room with a haze. In disbelief, he saw himself racing around the room in slow motion, shouting and screaming for Sarah.

Somehow, it didn't seem strange that he was watching himself watch himself ...

The dream flickered and changed.

Gordon next saw himself sitting at Dragnorr's computer station typing furiously.

The buzzing grew so loud he couldn't think ...

He was running ... running ... always running ...

"Gordon ... listen to me carefully ... " Hylrada whispered from far, far away.

Everything shimmered with millions of twinkling lights.

And suddenly, the world around him became real again.

"Listen to Tom -- believe him!" Hylrada said clearly.

He stared down at Tom.

"You told me we must get out of here when the explosions started! You said the safety system was disabled and each bolt of lightning from outside would now surge through the grid!" Tom yelled urgently

Gordon shook his head in an attempt to clear his mind from the mental fog.

"Boy!" Gordon shouted. "I never told you any such thing!"

"Yes, you did! You were with me, just before you came in with Miss Sarah and all those creatures from the other door!"

"What?"

"And you loosened my shackles and told me to stay still until you began fighting."

Gordon felt the world spinning around him.

"You told me to grab the Stunner, stun them, and toss that staff at you."

Gordon clenched Tom tighter.

"You say it was me?"

"Yes, that was why I was so shocked when you walked in the other door only seconds after you left by the other!"

Gordon froze.

And then he knew.

"Let's go, Tom. We've got to get out of here! If I said this place is about to blow up, I must be right!"

"What?" Tom's expression grew very perplexed.

"Where's this secret way?" Gordon peered intently at the boy.

"You said it was in the corner -- there would be a pad on the wall."

Gordon ran over and immediately saw it.

He stood right before it and stared.

An overwhelming sense of déjà vu gripped him.

He had seen this pad before!

And with an eerie shimmering, the pad wavered as if no longer solid and real. Gordon groaned as he felt the dizziness filling his head again.

The buzzing in his earpiece now rose suddenly in volume.

And just as suddenly, Hylrada was speaking in super slow motion.

He blinked rapidly and opened his eyes.

And without the slightest hesitation, he typed in the command to open it.

"How did I know that?" He stared at his fingers.

"Run, quickly!" Hylrada's voice was now normal as he urged him to action.

"You're back, Hylrada," Gordon said.

"I never left, Gordon. You're the one who left."

Gordon shook his head as he ran down the passageway.

The explosions grew more intense with each black lightning bolt that struck the domes. Debris fell from the ceiling all around them, causing them to sidestep or jump over pieces that fell in their path.

They ran through the entry room between the domed buildings and then onto the walkway above the great room that had been filled with row after row of Anon watching time portals.

The room below was a jumbled mess of debris and broken equipment and empty of any movement. The Anon had left already.

Gordon glanced up as they came to the door that led to the room with the window by which they had first gained entrance.

The inner curve of the vast dome ceiling glowed as bolts of black electricity leaped into the air above them. To his shock, he saw the entire dome shift as debris shot into the middle of the room from all four walls.

"It's collapsing!" Gordon shouted.

They ran faster and sprinted toward the window.

Seconds later, they jumped through the window. They didn't slow down as more thunder boomed and shook the ground and more debris rained down around them. They kept running, realizing everything was about to collapse in total destruction behind them.

Finally, Gordon looked back.

At just that moment, the huge steel dome collapsed straight down in a cloud of smoke as the first structure collapsed.

It started a chain reaction.

The second dome collapsed seconds later, and then a huge blast of black lightning struck the dome of the largest building.

For one entire second, the entire dome glowed black.

And then it started to collapse inexorably.

"Run!" Gordon shouted.

Gordon and Tom raced down the ravine as fast as they could run.

All around them, pieces of concrete and other debris showered down as the string of explosions grew to a deafening roar.

All the explosions suddenly grew together into one, mighty blast.

Gordon pushed Tom down just as the blast wave hit them.

He felt himself flung against the other side of the ravine.

And everything went dark.

Chapter Twenty-Seven

Gordon opened his eyes.

"Mr. Smith, are you all right?" Tom bent over him.

"Um ... yes." He felt around his body. Nothing important was missing or severely bent out of place.

He slowly stood up.

"Yes, I seem to be in one piece." He patted the boy's shoulder.

He looked up and saw three huge columns of smoke rising high into the lavender sky.

"They're gone, completely destroyed!" Tom gasped.

"Right. Well, we need to find my Transporter and get out of here."

They ran down the maze of ravines while Gordon adjusted the hand-held sensor. He found the location of the stolen Transporter and ran toward those coordinates.

But, when they arrived, it was gone.

"Gone again?" Gordon rubbed his face in puzzlement.

"What's gone?" Tom asked.

"My Transporter. It's been stolen ... again." Gordon walked in circles around the spot where it had last been. He shook his head all the while. "Well, whatever happened, it's gone again."

His fingers danced over the hand-held. He held it up and turned to face eastward.

"Yes!" he cried happily when the device beeped.

"What's that then?" Tom asked.

"My other Transporter is still there. Let's go."

They ran through the ravines at breakneck speed. Ten minutes later, they arrived.

Gordon pulled the leather string up from around his neck and held the key up to the air.

The door appeared.

Gordon and Tom stepped quickly inside.

"Wow!" Tom gasped in surprise as he looked around.

Gordon ran over to the Navigation station and typed furiously.

Once again, Gordon felt the dizziness return.

"Gordon ... " Hylrada's voice grew distant again. And somehow, there was an echo to it now.

"Not now, Hylrada!" Gordon said with a commanding tone.

"It's ... too ... dangerous ... " The echo intensified as Hylrada's voice faded to nothing.

Gordon checked the temporal and spatial settings.

As he looked, it seemed the numbers changed.

He closed his eyes and looked again.

The numbers were different. Or were they?

He double-checked his calculations.

No, they were correct.

"Hang on, Tom. This is going to be a rough ride!"

Tom grabbed hold of a steel post as he stared in amazement.

"Here we go!"

The buzzing in his earpiece now became an angry swarm of bees.

Gordon's stomach cramped so hard and so painfully that he bent over double and gasped out loud.

"Mr. Smith!"

Gordon looked up.

Everything grew fluid and slightly out of focus. As he stared around in slow motion, the interior of the Transporter grew dream-like. It seemed that millions of tiny stars began to twinkle.

"Mr. Smith!"

Gordon shook himself.

He looked around; everything was solid again.

The Transporter shook violently as it landed too hard.

Gordon fell to the floor, as did Tom.

"Where are we?" Tom asked fearfully.

Gordon slowly got up and held up the key.

He stepped through and found himself inside a bedroom. He walked over to the window and looked down upon a street filled with people on their way to work in the early morning light.

"London." He turned and smiled at Tom. "We're back in London, lad."

Tom looked out the window.

"I've never been so glad to see it in my entire life!" Tom cried joyfully.

Gordon's entire body suddenly ached horribly, as if some invisible vise held him and was now being slowly turned in order to crush him to death. He fell against the wall and slowly crumpled to the floor.

Gordon groaned painfully.

"Gordon ... stop ... " Hylrada's faraway voice echoed strangely.

"What's wrong, sir?" Tom cried out clearly.

251

"Nothing, lad." Gordon stifled another groan. "Nothing. Now, listen to me ... "

"Yes, sir." Tom leaned closer.

"Go find William Shakespeare. He's back at his flat." Gordon grimaced as the pain overwhelmed him again.

"But, sir! You're hurt!"

"No, I'm not." Gordon groaned. He grasped Tom urgently by the arm. "You've got to run fast and find him. Go ... now!"

"And when I find him?"

Gordon paused.

And for a split second, the pain faded.

"Tell him you want to join his troupe -- you want to be an actor. Tell him ... I sent you."

Tom's face lit up.

"Right, I'll go find him."

Tom turned and ran out through the door.

The terrible pain returned with crushing ferocity.

He struggled to rise. Finally, he stood panting for breath as if he had just run for miles.

Gordon looked out at the street.

Something caught his attention, and he looked up several blocks.

He saw himself and Sarah running through the crowds with Rawf beside them.

Gordon turned and ran for the door. He raced down the stairs to the first floor and rushed out into the street filled with people.

"Watch yourself!"

Gordon ran right into two men, who pushed him back roughly.

He looked around.

Everything shimmered as if fluid.

And the terrible pressure crushed him again.

He ran.

People jumped aside as he ran blindly across the street. He tried to mutter apologies, but he couldn't speak. He waved his arms blindly as he ran faster and the people stared at him and stepped out of his way.

And right as he reached the middle of the street, he felt a strong urge to look over to the side.

Gordon saw himself looking back at him.

Gordon Smith stared at him in shock as Sarah Nightingale turned toward him too.

He stumbled and almost fell.

He kept his face down, but even the cobblestone street wavered and shimmered as if it were fluid.

He ran and ran and ran.

Suddenly, he passed through a curtain of light.

His mind cleared in that very moment.

He was in the alley.

Gordon grabbed at the leather necklace and pulled the key out and pointed it. He ran toward the end of the alley.

A door appeared out of thin air.

He jumped inside.

The buzzing in his earpiece grew silent.

He looked around and breathed a sigh of relief. The incredible pain racking his body was gone. And best of all, everything was solid again.

Gordon raced over to the Navigation console and typed furiously.

He glanced over at another console.

It showed the alley outside.

And right then, Gordon Smith and Sarah Nightingale raced into view.

The pressure-filled pain gripped him again like a gigantic vise.

Gordon fell over the station as he typed the final coordinates.

He hit the lever to jump just as he collapsed into unconsciousness.

Chapter Twenty-Eight

He awoke with a start.

Gordon looked around in a daze. For a moment, he didn't know where he was. He felt a panic-stricken urge to run.

He stood up.

It all came flooding back into his mind.

Gordon checked the local time.

"Oh, no!" he cried.

He picked up his Stunner and felt his coat. His hand rubbed against the open gash where Dragnorr had ripped it. He flinched with the memory.

He reached further and felt the bulk of the Time Rod.

Gordon held up the key and raced outside.

Right above him, Dragnorr's domed laboratory rose like a dream.

He turned as a sound caught his attention.

Gordon paused, listening intently.

He heard himself talking to Sarah as they both approached.

Gordon turned and ran.

He made it to the base of the wall and quickly began his climb. A few minutes later, he lifted his leg up on the ledge, sat on the window opening while he twisted his body and then jumped inside.

He turned back and noticed the scuffmarks on the window ledge that he would find a few minutes later.

The ledge shimmered and waved in a surreal motion.

Gordon turned and ran across the room.

He knew exactly where he was going.

The great room with the dome roof stretched out before him. Down below, row after row after row of Anon sat staring at portals of time.

Gordon raced along the wall until he neared the corner where the passageway turned to go into the entrance room to the main building.

A noise distracted him from behind.

He glanced back and saw himself coming through the door of the first room.

Gordon ran quickly and dashed around the corner.

Of course, he already knew the Gordon behind him had caught the briefest glimpse as he ran out of sight.

It didn't matter.

He ran through the entrance foyer and carefully entered the main room.

But, instead of going right, as he originally did, he ran left toward the secret entrance to Dragnorr's inner lair.

Gordon went through the door and down the narrow passageway until he came to the stairs he knew he'd find. He quietly walked up to the door in the corner of the room that housed the Time Tunnel.

He stared at the keypad and realized he didn't know the code to open it!

"D-d-d-describe th-th-th-the pad-d-d-d," Hylrada said, his voice echoing strangely.

"Square pad with the numerals one through nine on the first three rows and a bottom row of zero, a double zero and a triple zero."

A low buzzing grew inside his earpiece. As it

did, he realized the pad swirled around and even the wall waved like a flag.

He blinked his eyes rapidly as he wavered unsteadily.

The buzzing grew deafening.

Gordon tapped it with his finger, as if such a simple trick would clear it up.

Hylrada's voice became discernable.

"Six, then three, then five, then six again.

Gordon typed the numbers.

A buzzer sounded

"Didn't work."

"Hang on," Hylrada said.

As he waited, Gordon fixed his gaze on the pad.

He knew he'd seen it before; he'd recognized it when he first escaped ... but he had jumped back in time and right 'now' -- the present -- it was several minutes before he would first see it ... but he still recognized it ... he had seen it before ... but his 'other self' would not see it for the first time for a few more minutes ... but he recognized it ... but not 'now', it was 'then' ... and somewhere in 'between' ... and in the 'future' he might not ...

He stared at the pad.

And with an eerie shimmering, the pad wavered as if no longer solid and real. Gordon groaned as he felt the dizziness filling his head again.

The buzzing in his earpiece rose suddenly in volume.

And just as suddenly, Hylrada was speaking in super slow motion.

He blinked rapidly and opened his eyes.

"Double zero ... then six ... then five ... then nine

257

... then one ... " Hylrada's voice was normal again.

"How do you know that?" Gordon asked.

"Alkir, from my temporal network. He's run across one when the Anon visited him. He actually sneaked inside the Anon's transporter for a look but had to figure out the code first. It was different than before, but Alkir's a natural hacker."

"Brilliant."

"Well, that was our fourth attempt -- we had to get it right soon -- or else ... "

"Fourth attempt? I only recall two?"

A strange static replaced the buzzing.

Gordon typed the numbers, and the door opened.

He carefully entered the room.

It was empty.

Gordon slipped through past the chair in the middle of the room and on to the door that opened to Dragnorr's lair.

He stopped and tried to listen at the door, but he couldn't hear anything. Gordon leaned against the cool metal and pressed his ear right on it. Now, he heard the voices clearly.

"They will come for the child," Dragnorr hissed vehemently.

"Dragnorr, one of our watchers has reported a disturbance in the ether almost two kilometers from us."

"Good, good!"

"We have cross-checked the data, and we suspect that even now Gordon Smith and Sarah Nightingale are inside."

"Then, let us go meet them."

"Where?"

"Oh, they're quite adept. We shall go meet them at the entrance of my lair. I'm sure they'll arrive quite soon now."

Gordon waited as the footsteps grew fainter.

After a pause, he heard the distinct sound of a door being shut.

Gordon opened the door where he'd been listening and rushed inside.

"Mr. Smith!" Tom Walker said with surprise.

"Shhhhh." Gordon held a forefinger up to his mouth.

Quickly, he ran over to Dragnorr's computer station and sat down in front of the main console.

"Good, in his arrogance he has left his session running." Gordon grinned like a wolf.

He typed the commands that disabled all the safety mechanisms and allowed the full, unregulated strength of each lightning bolt striking each dome to surge throughout the entire power grid. The floods of electricity through the grid would grow more destructive with each lightning strike until everything was totally destroyed.

He added a timer loop that would tick down and finally execute the fatal command.

The command embedded in the loop was on the screen, but he did not execute it. Gordon rose quickly and walked over to Tom.

"Mr. Smith, I knew you'd come to get me." Tom laughed.

"Yes, Tom. Now, you must listen carefully and do exactly as I tell you. All right?" Gordon peered at the boy resolutely.

"Yes, sir."

"Good lad. Now, I'm going to release the lock that holds your wrists. However, you must act as if you are still bound tight." Gordon quickly worked the bands holding the boy's wrists until both clicked open. He then pushed them closer together so at a glance no one would notice they were open.

"Got it?"

"Yes, sir. But, what will you be doing?"

"I've got some things still to do. I've got to destroy this entire facility and rid ourselves of that monster. Right?"

"Yes, sir."

"Good. Now, here's my final commands."

Gordon quickly informed the boy not to release himself until he saw him, Gordon Smith, fighting with the Anon holding him. And that would be after Miss Sarah was taken away. And last, when the explosions began, he must remind him -- Gordon Smith -- that they had to leave immediately, or else they would perish in the final explosion.

"Why do I need to remind you?"

Gordon paused. He flashed a smile.

"Because I get so busy I forget things like that."

Tom's mouth dropped open in surprise.

"Now then, you have it down, right?"

"Yes, sir."

"I'm going to sit at this station over here and wait until I hear footsteps approaching. That will be Dragnorr coming back. Just before he enters, I'm going to set off a command and then clear the screen so it runs in the background."

"Got it," Tom said dutifully.

"One last thing, Tom. When the explosions start and we rush inside the room with the Time Tunnel, don't forget to remind me that we need to escape through the secret passage located at the far corner of the room. There's a keypad on the wall to open the door -- which won't look like a door. Got it?"

"Yes!"

Gordon sat down at the console.

"Sir?"

"Yes, Tom."

"Don't you think you should see a doctor about your memory problems? It seems odd that I need to remind you of such important details, sir."

Gordon chuckled.

"Yes, right after we get back to London, eh?"

"Yes, sir."

They waited in silence.

After a few moments, the sound of approaching footsteps came to their ears.

Gordon turned to Tom and nodded.

The boy nodded back.

Gordon typed the command and started the timer. He quickly cleared the screen with the command running in the background now.

He got up and ran to the door that led back into the Time Tunnel.

He stopped right at the door and snapped his fingers.

"Tom, don't be surprised ... "

The door at the other end opened.

Gordon rushed inside and shut the door behind.

He stood a moment at the door and listened. After a few moments, he heard muffled voices coming close. Soon he recognized Dragnorr speaking. And then, he heard the curtain pushed aside.

"Tom!" Sarah cried out.

"Miss Sarah!" Tom cried joyfully.

Gordon heard Tom gasp out loud and realized that the boy had just seen his other self.

Gordon turned around and surveyed the room. Up till now, he had known exactly where to go and what to do.

But now, he had to figure out how to rescue Sarah ...

Chapter Twenty-Nine

Gordon pulled out his Stunner.

From the other room, he heard himself speaking.

The room around him shimmered and waved in a surreal, fluid motion. He fell against the chair where Sarah would soon be strapped. He fought against the dizziness that now rushed through his mind in waves.

He had to get ready ...

Gordon stumbled forward until he found an area behind one of the computer stations where he could hide, but even as he fell to the floor out of sight, the room continued to shimmer and wave.

How could he rescue Sarah in this condition? He wouldn't be able to shoot straight and stun anybody, much less rescue her.

Gordon closed his eyes and concentrated.

Now, his body burned as if in a terrible fever, and an aching filled every part of his body until he couldn't bear it any longer.

He groaned out loud.

"*Gordon, listen to me carefully.*"

Hylrada's voice reverberated strangely, almost as if he spoke from deep, deep inside a tunnel.

And there was the oddest echoing ...

"Gordon?"

"Hylrada ... your voice is so strange now." Gordon coughed as the pain intensified.

"Gordon, you're in a bad place. And worse, you're in a bad time."

Gordon groaned and collapsed on the floor.

Somewhere in the background, he heard a door

open.

Or was his mind playing tricks?

In the fog of pain, he heard a woman's voice.

"Let me go! Stop it!"

Yes, it definitely sounded like a woman. It even sounded a bit like Sarah ...

"Gordon?"

He opened his eyes and stared as the entire world swirled like a kaleidoscope.

"It's so pretty ... " Gordon whispered.

"Gordon, hold your breath."

He laughed -- well, inside his mind he laughed. But, he did as he was told. Gordon Smith dutifully held his breath.

"Good ... keep holding it and listen carefully."

He nodded.

"You are in a time loop and, worse, you are in very close proximity to your other self. The normal space/time universe at the sub-molecular level is attempting to compensate now that a once-unique temporal/spatial event is compromised. And your mind is hallucinating because space/time is starting to collapse around you ... "

"Is that bad?" Gordon asked in a whisper.

"Please be quiet -- there are two Anon near you!"

He nodded.

"Yes, it is bad," Hylrada whispered.

"It sounds bad," Gordon whispered in reply.

"Quiet!"

He nodded.

"Are you still holding your breath?"

Gordon took a deep breath, closed his mouth

and nodded although there was no way Hylrada could see him.

"Listen! Keep your eyes closed and hold your breath for one full minute. I will tell you when you reach one minute. Your mind will slowly clear as you block out the visual phenomena and you'll be able to function for a very short time when you do open your eyes.

He lay on the floor in the fetal position with his eyes shut as he held his breath. Seconds passed ... or it seemed that seconds passed ... And time passed ... Or did years pass?

Deep inside his mind, he suddenly remembered his name.

He liked that -- always good to know one's own name.

His jumbled thoughts slowed, and he remembered he was on a rescue mission ... yes, he had to rescue Sarah Nightingale. He clearly remembered that part now. And more! He remembered he was in the Time Tunnel room of Dragnorr's laboratory. The Anon had just brought Sarah inside and strapped her to the chair. In the next few moments they would back off and Dragnorr would flip the switch and send Sarah shooting off ...

Gordon opened his eyes.

"Now," Hylrada said.

He let out his breath. As he breathed in, he glanced up.

The world still shimmered and wavered as if fluid -- but no longer like the vortex of a whirlpool.

Two Anon stood right above him with their

backs to him.

Gordon pointed his Stunner and fired twice.

One of the Anon fell while the other turned in shock and looked down at him.

"Oops, I missed one."

The Anon's figure wavered and shimmered.

He fired three times -- just to the right, just to the left and directly at the Anon.

One of his shots hit true, and the Anon finally fell over.

"Get up -- you've only got seconds left to free Sarah!" Hylrada whispered urgently.

Gordon stood up.

He turned; Sarah Nightingale was strapped to a chair in the middle of the room, screaming frantically.

Suddenly, the swirling coalesced, and everything seemed real again.

"Sarah."

"Gordon?" she whispered in shock. "How can you be in here, when you're out there?" She nodded at the closed door.

From outside the door, the distinct sound of fighting came to their ears.

Gordon stumbled forward and began tearing at the straps.

The sound of a powerful engine quickly increasing in power filled their ears.

"Get me free! I hear the Time Tunnel revving up," Sarah said with urgent fervor.

Gordon pulled at the straps faster.

The noises outside the door stopped.

He freed one hand and turned to the other.

"Control him!" Dragnorr hissed from the other side of the door.

Gordon realized the monster was about to hit the button -- and it would send both of them lost into time!

He freed her other hand, grabbed her and jumped toward the fallen Anon just as a bright flash of light erupted from the other end of the room ...

Chapter Thirty

The light hurt his eyes even with them clenched tightly shut.

Slowly, the burning light faded, as did the high-pitched engine noise.

He opened his eyes and found himself staring into Sarah's bright blue eyes.

She clenched her fist and hit his arm as hard as she could.

"Ow!"

"Next time be a bit quicker, Gordon Smith!"

The sound of a Time Rod shooting its beam of electricity came clearly through the door.

"What was that?" Sarah asked.

"I just shot Dragnorr somewhere off into time with a Time Rod."

"You did *what*? How can that ... "

Gordon pressed his fingers on her lips.

"Hush -- the other me might hear you. He thinks you're gone, and he's going to rush in here in a few seconds and find us both here if we don't leave right now."

Sarah's eyes widened in fear.

He removed his fingers.

"Would that be bad -- if he finds us in here?" she asked.

"Last time it happened, my rogs all exploded," Hylrada said with a serious tone.

Gordon and Sarah jumped up.

And the vortex filled his vision again. As he took a step and stumbled, Sarah reached out and grabbed him.

"What's wrong with you?" she whispered.

"Sarah, you'll have to guide him," Hylrada advised.

"Which way?"

"Straight ahead, toward the corner. You'll find a number pad on the wall."

Gordon felt himself being pushed quite roughly.

He stumbled over his feet and almost fell again.

"Gordon ... close your eyes and hold your breath."

Gordon did just that.

"Hold on ... "

Inside his mind, he remembered his name.

"Open your eyes."

He saw the familiar number pad again.

Gordon punched the right code, and the secret door slid silently open.

"Go, Sarah!" Hylrada's tone was frantic now.

He felt Sarah put her arms around him and push him forward.

Gordon's face was suddenly mashed against a hard wall.

"Ow!"

"Sorry."

He felt himself shifted over and looked up.

The secret door was sliding shut, and as he watched, the door on the other side of the room began to open.

The vortex returned with a vengeance.

And was replaced by darkness as the door slid completely shut.

"The farther away you get Gordon from his other self, the better for his health and his mind,"

Hylrada urged.

"Gordon!"

He felt Sarah pull him up.

"Yes, dear?"

"We've got to run -- fast!"

Sarah turned him around and held him up steady. An instant later, he felt the palm of her hands slap hard against his butt.

Gordon ran.

And immediately, the pain lessened.

He ran faster.

They ran down the long corridor of the walkway to another door and sprinted through.

Gordon recognized the entry room between the domed buildings.

They ran and entered the first domed room with its rows and rows of Anon watching time portals.

But now, there was complete chaos below.

Thousands of Anon were fleeing for the exits while debris exploded from all four walls under the weight of the great steel dome above as it shifted with each blast of black lightning. A terrible grinding noise filled the air as the entire building began to slowly collapse around them.

Down below, showers of sparks erupted from hundreds of computer stations, and the glowing curtains of time portals flicked off by the dozens all around the great room. Everywhere they looked, destruction erupted

"Run!" Hylrada shouted.

Gordon felt his mind clearing even more. The terrible aching was now a distant fog.

They ran across the room toward the window by

which they first gained entrance.

A few minutes later, they ran down the nearest ravine toward the Time Transporter.

Sarah pulled out her key and held it up.

The outline of a door shimmered in the air and suddenly grew solid. They ran inside.

Gordon fell into the nearest chair, panting from his exertions.

Sarah ran over to the navigation station as Rawf barked happily in greeting.

"Rawf, stop barking. I've got to think," Sarah cried out.

"What now?" Gordon asked Hylrada.

"You've got to return to London, right at the very time you first left to chase Dragnorr."

"*Why?*" Sarah and Gordon shouted together.

"There is a temporal disturbance that is growing exponentially with each passing minute. It is so powerful it is shifting the earth's mantle below, and it will soon trigger an earthquake powerful enough to devastate all of London."

"*What?*"

"Yes, you've got to get the duplicate Time Transporter out of there within two minutes of your initial departure."

Gordon groaned as he rolled his eyes.

"It will be dangerous," Hylrada added.

"I realize that -- when we arrive, there will be *three* of me in those moments of time!"

"And two of me!" Sarah said with shock and surprise.

"It will be very dangerous."

Gordon and Sarah exchanged glances.

271

"What do we need to do?"

Chapter Thirty-One

Gordon and Sarah stepped outside the Time Transporter.

They were in a second-story room above the early morning streets of London filled with people. The clatter of horse's hooves on cobblestone along with the murmuring of the crowds outside emanated into the room through the window.

Together, they slowly crept to the window and stood on each side.

Gordon nodded at Sarah.

They both pulled back the curtains and looked down on the street below.

People walked quickly along the street in both directions as they began a new day.

Gordon and Sarah searched quickly, looking first one direction and then the other along the busy street as they got their bearings.

They saw themselves.

Sarah gasped as she held the curtain.

"I see myself running with you up the street!" Sarah said in disbelief.

Suddenly, the street wavered and became fluid. The people upon the wavering road continued walking the surreal twists and curves as if it were normal. Even the buildings twisted with a dream-like quality, and everything -- the sky, the clouds, the trees -- grew fluid and shimmered.

The dizziness filled his mind so intensely it hit him like a tidal wave. Gordon swooned and fell against the wall. Drops of sweat poured down his face as his body temperature grow unbearably hot.

He felt as if he would catch fire any second.

He reached for his throat, struggling to breathe, and the fever burned so hot his shirt grew wet.

"Gordon! What's happening?"

Sarah's voice sounded so far away ...

"Listen to me ... Gordon ... Sarah ... "

He heard Hylrada's distant voice echoing strangely as if from inside a dream.

"Both of you ... close your eyes and hold your breath."

Gordon felt his mind slowing down. It felt as if he were falling off a high cliff into nothingness, but he wasn't afraid. In fact, he yearned for it.

As he fell, he discovered he could focus his thoughts and he remembered why they were there.

And best of all, he remembered his name.

"Okay, check the window -- carefully."

Gordon opened his eyes and saw Sarah sitting on the floor on the other side of the window. She blinked her eyes as if awakening from sleep. She looked over at him and smiled.

Together, they looked out.

And in the street below, they saw Gordon Smith and Sarah Nightingale suddenly look directly up at them.

Gordon felt his heart pounding against his chest as his body filled with the same, terrible waves of pain. He looked to his right.

"Sarah, look there," Gordon said with a dreadful hush.

In a crowd of people, a second Gordon Smith ran toward the alley.

They both pushed the curtains shut across the

window.

"We're all out there," Gordon said with a slightly desperate tone.

"Good, close your eyes and hold your breath again."

Time seemed to stand still for Gordon as his thoughts slowed. He held his breath comfortably -- almost too comfortably.

"Now, time to get out of there!" Hylrada said urgently.

Gordon realized he was again sitting on the floor with his head against the wall as if he had been sleeping.

"What now?" he asked.

"Gordon, get in the Time Transporter and dial it to jump to London, June twenty-first, 1813."

"Right."

"Sarah, you will go into the next room and take the Time Transporter that the second Gordon Smith -- the one running into the alley to steal its twin -- left behind. Jump to the same time."

Gordon tried to stand but he couldn't quite remember how to do that particular exercise somehow.

So, he crawled.

"Let me help you."

He looked up, and Sarah smiled down at him.

She helped him up and they took a few steps forward. Sarah reached inside his wet shirt and pulled up the key hanging around his neck.

The door appeared, and she helped him inside.

He sat at the navigation station and punched in the coordinates.

"Good, darling," Sarah said as her eyes sparkled at him.

He watched as she went back to the door.

And just before she walked through, she turned back to him.

"I love you, Gordon Smith."

Chapter Thirty-Two

Gordon sat inside the Time Transporter.

With each passing second, the terrible ache that throbbed painfully in every fiber of his body lessened.

It couldn't fade fast enough for his liking.

He glanced around as the door opened.

Gordon groaned dramatically.

Sarah walked inside.

Just the sight of her smiling face and her blue eyes made his heart beat faster -- in a good way.

And the exhilaration of her touch made the pain fade even faster.

"Are you all right?" Sarah placed her hand softly on Gordon's forehead.

"I am, now that you're here."

"You feel like you've got a fever." She looked at him with concern.

"I feel like I've been stabbed." Gordon grimaced as he bent over with his arms around his waist. He groaned louder.

"Sounds like you're constipated to me."

Gordon glanced up quickly with a piercing expression.

"Just trying to lighten things up. After all, laughter is the best medicine." Sarah smiled brightly.

Gordon put his head back down and let out a long, low groan.

"Hmmm, yes. Like a really, *really* bad case -- totally clogged up. That would be my guess just by the agonizing sound alone."

277

"Right." Gordon rocked back and forth as he held himself tighter. "I can see how you might confuse the two, since both would cause the sufferer to elicit terrible sounds due to the severe and excruciating abdominal pains racking one's body."

Sarah sat down beside him. She peered intently at him, but Gordon continued to stare straight down at the ground. She put her arm around his shoulders and squeezed him lovingly.

Gordon looked up.

"You came back for me." Sarah's eyes sparkled as she smiled. "I'll never forget that, Gordon. I truly never will."

Gordon smiled. And immediately a painful expression replaced it, but he recovered and looked deeply into her blue eyes.

"I'll always come back for you, Sarah Nightingale."

"I know," she whispered.

Gordon felt an overwhelming desire to kiss her.

He looked down at her lips and slowly drew closer until he felt her warm breath caress his face. He closed his eyes. And as their lips touched ever so softly, the sensation sent an electric thrill throughout his entire body.

"How is he?" Hylrada's tone was full of concern.

Gordon and Sarah separated quickly at the sudden interruption. They shared a smile for a moment before answering.

"I think the fever is passing -- each time I check he feels cooler." Sarah took a deep breath and stood up.

"Good. Gordon, let me ask you a few

278

questions."

"Right, go ahead." Gordon stretched, trying to work out the pain that was still fading throughout his muscles.

"Where are you?"

"Let's see, that might be a difficult one ... London in the year 1813 ... the month is June. Now the date, hmmm, well, that I'm not sure ... "

"No, no. Where or what are you presently sitting inside?"

"Oh yes, that. I'm sitting inside a Time Transporter."

"Good. Who are you?"

"Let's see, last time I checked, I was still Gordon Smith."

"Fine. And what animal is that wagging his four tails and panting excitedly."

"That's your rog, Rawf."

"Excellent. Last, how do you feel?"

"I feel terrible, but that's a vast improvement on how I felt before we jumped."

"Do you remember what just happened to you?"

"Sort of." Gordon looked up at Sarah, who smiled back at him. "I think we chased Dragnorr back to his laboratory and we had quite a time of it. In fact, I had to go back in time again and rescue Sarah."

"Well then, I think you'll survive."

"I'm glad to hear that!" Gordon laughed.

"But that was the weirdest thing," Sarah said with a shake of her head. "Seeing ourselves like that."

"That was a bit odd." Gordon agreed.

"Some kind of time loop you think?" Sarah looked over at the console where Hylrada's visage smiled.

"Right, Hylrada. What exactly did happen to us?" Gordon looked from Sarah back to Hylrada's visage on the console.

"You just came out of a ... *triple time loop*." Hylrada's six ears wiggled as he nodded with an aura of pride.

"A triple time loop, eh?" Gordon rubbed his chin in thought.

"Sounds like something done off a diving board." Sarah chuckled.

"With a one and half twist at the end?" Gordon added quickly with a smile and a twinkle in his green eyes.

"Where did you learn about triple time loops?" Sarah asked.

"Oh, I just made it up. Just now, actually." Hylrada smiled.

"Did you?" Gordon laughed.

"Yet, it does fit the phenomena quite succinctly, if I say so myself." Hylrada straightened up in his chair and brushed the fur on his cheek with an air of dignified grace.

"I guess this was your first time observing such a thing -- this triple time loop?" Sarah sat against the console and crossed her arms. Her sandy blonde hair fell around her shoulders as she waited.

"Uh ... yes, it was. And I must say it was a most amazing spectacle indeed."

"What now?" Gordon grimaced as another wave of pain swept through him, although the pain was indeed lessening.

"Give yourself some time to recuperate first. After that, you and Sarah will need to jump back and visit Shakespeare one last time."

"And why is that?" Sarah asked.

"You must ensure the influence of Dragnorr on Shakespeare has been negated and he and his men intend to dismantle the theater and rebuild it as the Globe."

"And ensure the timeline of Earth is once again intact and the future unchanged."

"Yes."

"Right. Well, I can think of nothing with better recuperative powers than sharing a few pints of good ale with William Shakespeare." Gordon smiled.

"Some rest for you first, before any ale," Sarah counseled.

"A good night's rest first."

"No hurry either, Gordon. Rest a few days. You and Sarah can always jump back to the same morning you left him. He'll never know you've been away that long."

"Yes, this time traveling does have its benefits." Gordon chuckled.

"As long as you refrain from meeting yourself!" Hylrada added.

Chapter Thirty-Three

The air was punctuated by raucous laughter amid the happy babble of folk gathered inside the pub that cold winter night. At every table, smiling faces multiplied the jovial spirit that now permeated the candle-lit atmosphere and added to the pleasant warmth given off by the great room's crackling fire. The constant din grew so loud that everyone was forced to hold their heads close together in order to hear their table-mates' words.

Gordon Smith and Sarah Nightingale sat among the happy throng gathered at the 'Three-legged Dog' along with William Shakespeare. The three sat at a table next to a dark-timbered wall.

Gordon leaned toward Shakespeare and spoke in a near shout.

"So then, what have you and the rest of the Chamberlain's Men decided?" Gordon sat back and drank from his pint of ale with great appreciation.

Sarah leaned over the table as she looked deeply at Shakespeare.

"Desperate times require desperate actions." Shakespeare raised his pint.

"Here, here!" Sarah drank deeply of her ale.

"You're going to dismantle 'The Theater' then?" Gordon took his hand and placed it over Sarah's hand.

"It's kind of sad in a way," Shakespeare said reflectively. "The first plays by Thomas Kyd, Christopher Marlowe and myself were performed in that playhouse where it stands on High Street. Ah, so many memories. And so many faces gone, never to be seen again."

"Change is never easy," Sarah said. "And yet, the future of your new playhouse may prove even more memorable. And perhaps even greater plays shall be performed within its walls."

"Here, here." Gordon took a strong pull of his ale.

"May your words prove prophetic, dear woman. Yes, two days from now, we will march with the carpenters. We'll take the swords and spears we use in our mock combat so we can intimidate anyone who might try to stop us. And thus, we will stand guard as they dismantle it board by board, after which we shall transport it so as to be constructed into a new theater when the weather turns mild once more with the coming of spring." Shakespeare smiled and nodded, as if treasuring some private dream.

"And, you will rebuild your new theater south of the Thames -- outside the jurisdiction of London proper."

"Yes."

Gordon cast a sly look at Sarah.

"And what shall you christen your new home?" Gordon asked with a smile.

"The Globe Theater."

Sarah laughed out loud as she slapped the table.

"So then, I will prophesy one better than Sarah. I will wager that the 'greatest' plays ever written by Master William Shakespeare shall be performed at your new home. And that the memories you create there shall indeed be the happiest of your entire life."

"May it even be so!" Shakespeare shouted.

They all took a drink together.

"How is Tom getting along with your company?" Sarah asked.

"The lad is bright, that one. I've decided to take him under my wing and teach him myself. He'll make a fine actor." Shakespeare smiled.

Gordon leaned closer to him. "Perhaps Tom Walker will play the lead in one of your future plays?"

"I have many in my heart yearning to be written!"

"And the world will be a better place because of them," Sarah said.

They all took another pull from their mugs.

"And what about you two?" Shakespeare wiped some ale from his chin.

Gordon and Sarah glanced at each other and smiled.

"We'll come around from time to time, I think."

"I hope you will come this time next year." Shakespeare smiled with a merry twinkle in his eyes as he stroked his short beard.

"You'll have a new play?"

"Hamlet."

"Oh!" Gordon coughed and sputtered his ale. He pummeled his chest to clear the drink he had just tried to breathe.

"I see," Gordon said at last. "So, you've started writing it, I guess?"

"Oh yes, and I finished the scene using that thought-provoking line you uttered the other night."

"*What?*" Sarah stared accusingly at Gordon.

Gordon took another pull of ale in reflective silence.

"What line did you utter for Shakespeare?" She finally asked.

Shakespeare held his almost empty pint up in the air as his face softened as if in the deepest contemplation.

"*To be, or not to be. That ... is the question.*" Shakespeare spoke the words with a slow and deliberate cadence.

Sarah clenched her fist and hit Gordon's arm.

"Owww!"

Gordon pulled away from her and rubbed his sore arm.

"You know, dear Sarah, you've got to stop doing that. I've got a bruise on my arm that hasn't healed in two weeks."

"Well, what are you doing mucking about with the timeline like that! Helping Shakespeare write Hamlet ... no telling what horrific changes you might have started. You may have changed the future completely!"

Shakespeare stared at both of them dumbfounded.

"Ah, you know women." Gordon nodded at Shakespeare. "Always exaggerating."

Shakespeare roared with laughter.

Gordon leaned forward and spoke in a voice so only the three of them could hear.

"Do me a favor, William. You wrote that line, lad. It's yours -- all Shakespeare. No need to ever mention me." Gordon waved his hands in the air and sat back in his chair.

"What modesty!" Shakespeare bowed his head slightly in appreciation. "But even if the entire world thinks I wrote every word -- you and I will know your contribution."

Gordon laughed out loud.

"You will come to see it performed, then?" Shakespeare asked.

"Absolutely! Sarah and I will keep tabs on the schedule at 'The Globe', and when we see the advertisement for the first performance of a new play by William Shakespeare entitled *Hamlet* -- we shall be in the audience."

"We'll be there -- right up front with the groundlings!" Sarah added with a laugh.

The evening and the happy talk and the golden ale continued unabated for many uncounted moments.

Later that evening, Gordon and Sarah stepped inside the Time Transporter.

"Shakespeare is fun kind of fellow, don't you think?" Gordon asked as he sat in his favorite chair in the corner.

"Witty and charming," Sarah said as she sat down in a chair opposite him. "And a keen sense of humor."

"We'll have to come round often."

"Hello, Gordon and Sarah." Hylrada's face appeared on the console.

"Hello, Hylrada. How's the timeline and the universe doing tonight?" Gordon laughed.

"There are no disturbances of which I am aware, nor any reports by anyone else in my network of associates spread across time and space."

"Then the universe is safe for tonight."

"Uh, Hylrada?" Sarah asked inquisitively.

"Yes, Sarah."

"What do you think happened to Dragnorr? Do you think we'll see him again?"

"Gordon rashly used a Time Rod on him. There is no telling where in space and time he wound up, I'm afraid."

"That'll take him a while to figure out. I don't think we'll see him for quite a long time, eh?" Gordon chuckled.

"That is a fair assumption. However, Dragnorr is quite clever. I feel sure he will figure a way out from wherever he's trapped. We will have to prepare for that eventuality."

"And what about us?" Sarah asked. "I mean, Dragnorr admitted he changed the timeline and somehow prevented both of us from being born."

Sarah looked from Gordon back to Hylrada.

"Can we find a way to undo it?"

"That will be difficult, especially since we can't question Dragnorr for more details," Hylrada said.

"He mentioned Folkestone -- I take it that was either the city name or perhaps the project's name?" Gordon asked hopefully.

"Yes, that is an important detail."

"And there were seven of us on the original team. Dragnorr didn't say he killed them -- perhaps they're also trapped in time somewhere?" Sarah sat up straight. "If we find one of them, perhaps they can help us figure out what to do?"

"That is quite possible. At least they will know enough details that we could pinpoint the exact time period when Folkestone was initiated." Hylrada nodded.

"But, we really need Dragnorr." Gordon sighed.

"Yes, he knows exactly what changes he initiated. If we know those details, we may find a way to undo the damage." Hylrada purred soothingly.

"Time travel is fraught with danger. You are exactly right." Sarah stood up and walked over to the console as Hylrada watched. "It's too dangerous. I think in a strange, selfish kind of way, Dragnorr was actually protecting the timelines."

"What do you mean?" Hylrada asked with surprise.

"I mean, he prevented others from discovering and using time travel. If there are too many traveling here and there, think how great the odds are that something will change even accidentally with all that time traveling."

Sarah glanced at Gordon with a stern expression.

"Look how Gordon helped Shakespeare out with his most famous play -- giving him it's most famous line -- perhaps the most famous line of any play of all time!"

"Now, hang on. It was all unintentional, wasn't it?" Gordon felt hurt.

"That's exactly what I mean. Think of all the potential damage that could be done simply by accident -- simply speaking the wrong thing at the wrong time!"

"But, Dragnorr was doing more that simply preventing others from developing the capability to travel through time. He was greedily and without remorse making changes to suit his selfish purposes." Hylrada shook his head with disapproval.

"You told us before that we were the first humans you ever found traveling through the ether of time and space, right?" Gordon sat upright in his chair.

"Yes."

"How many others -- non-humans -- have you ever detected traveling through time?" Sarah asked.

"A mere handful."

"See, it may not be a good thing if thousands started jumping about. Perhaps it should be controlled?" Sarah crossed her arms.

"Or monitored?" Gordon walked over beside Sarah.

"Yes, Dragnorr had thousands of Anon monitoring time portals for disturbances in the ether that would signal someone was attempting time travel. Perhaps you and the others in your network should monitor for the same thing?"

"In a way, we do that already. However, I see your point. Perhaps I can create some code that will monitor greater stretches of time automatically and signal me upon detection!"

"Good idea, Hylrada. You can pass that technology on to the other members of your little network, and all of you can keep a keen eye out for trouble."

"And, what will we do if we detect trouble?" Hylrada asked simply.

"Why, Sarah and I are the only time travelers

I'm aware of at the moment. I suppose you'll call on us, and we'll jump over and investigate." Gordon flashed a wide smile at Hylrada.

"A capital idea." Hylrada smiled in return.

"But, what about us -- personally?" Sarah asked with nervousness.

"Yes, I forgot that. We don't actually exist in normal space-time. What's to become of us if we can't find a way to undo Dragnorr's tampering?" Gordon's expression grew concerned as he ran his hand through his brown hair.

"Well, I have some good news and some bad news," Hylrada said matter-of-factly.

"Uh-oh, don't know if I like the sound of that," Gordon said quickly.

"The good news first?" Hylrada prompted.

"Right, let's have it."

"Since you only exist in the ether outside space and time, you may not age normally. And, my limited observations so far do confirm my theory that neither one of you are, in fact, aging at all. As far as I can tell."

Hylrada's vertical pupils dilated as he blinked several times.

"We won't grow old?" Gordon slapped his thigh with joy. "You mean, Sarah and I will be thirty years old -- forever?"

"Well, indefinitely, which could be the same thing," Hylrada said.

"Thirty years old?" Sarah said with an angry tone.

"Right, both of us will remain thirty years old ... on and on."

"I'll have you know, Gordon Smith, that I am only twenty-five years old and not a day older!" Her eyes narrowed dangerously.

He started to remind her that he did remember exactly how old she was -- but in a quick retrospective of careful analytic reasoning, taking into full account the feminine psyche and the age-old struggle of men trying to fully understand women's feelings and never, ever quite succeeding -- he decided the best course of action was not to correct her. After all, it was late and he was tired and there was no need to start a fuss he wouldn't win anyway -- even though the facts were on his side.

"Right ... so I'll be thirty years old forever and you'll be ... *twenty-five* -- forever."

"Well, that part doesn't sound bad at all." Sarah smiled confidently.

"What's the bad news?" Gordon asked with a chipper tone.

"You could disappear at any moment."

Gordon felt an electric shock of surprise surge throughout his body.

"Well now, that does sound a bit on the bad side of things," Gordon said thoughtfully.

"*What?*" Sarah shouted.

"It's only a theory at this point. I don't have all the facts gathered to make a firm conclusion.

"Perhaps we ought to continue with finding how to undo Dragnorr's tampering then?" Gordon suggested with a serious tone.

"Yes, I agree." Sarah closed her eyes.

"But, no need to worry unduly," Hylrada said

cheerfully.

"Easy for you to say -- you're not the one that might *spontaneously disappear* at a moment's notice," Sarah said in a tone edged with frustration.

"I think the odds of that are quite small. Here, I can provide some numbers ... "

"Hylrada!" Sarah shouted abruptly.

"Yes, Sarah?" Hylrada said sheepishly.

"How about just switching off for the night. You've told us enough theories for one evening. I'm sure I won't get a wink of sleep with what you've shared with us already!"

"Yes, right." Hylrada smiled. "Until tomorrow then."

The console flicked off.

Sarah shook her head as she began pacing around the room with a nervous air.

Gordon watched her a few moments before he spoke.

"Sarah, dear. Don't worry too much. We'll figure this out. We've done all right so far."

She shook her head.

Gordon noticed the tears running down her cheeks.

"Now, now, Sarah."

He walked over and embraced her tenderly.

They held each other close for a long time -- just holding onto each other. The seconds passed in a kind of shared melancholy mixed with mutual caring.

Finally, Gordon raised his head from off Sarah's shoulder. Her face was still resting against his shoulder as he caressed her back comfortingly.

"You are the only constant in my life, dear Sarah. In all my memories -- we are together. I love you, Sarah Nightingale. I'll always love you. And I want to love you forever."

Sarah pulled back enough so she could search his face.

He smiled.

Sarah smiled in return.

Gordon pulled her back into his arms, and they embraced with an urgent tenderness.

"Maybe you ought to marry her?" Hylrada smiled with his six ears wiggling excitely.

"What?" Gordon looked over at the console and Hylrada's face.

"Have you been peeping on us?" Sarah said with rising anger.

"Oh, no! Not at all. I just remembered something else and thought I ought to tell you before you went to sleep. I only caught that last part -- about you loving her and all."

"The good part, eh." Gordon smiled at Sarah.

Sarah put her arms around Gordon's waist and pulled him close against her.

"Yes, Gordon Smith. If you really, *really* love me, why don't we just go ahead and get married?" She looked deeply into Gordon's eyes as her lips came close to his.

He felt the warmth of her breath caress him. He felt her closeness stir his deepest emotions like a fire. Gordon looked deeply into her clear, blue eyes until it seemed he fell into them.

But as his heart raced out of control, another feeling exploded. And now his entire being was filled with equal parts of exhilaration and fear.

Fear or ...

Yes, he recognized this new emotion wrestling inside him as a tidal wave of pure panic. And he knew what had brought it on -- the thought of the 'm' word. After all, getting married was so ... so ... permanent.

"It's not that simple for us -- since we don't really exist," Gordon countered.

"We exist, Gordon. We exist enough. Come on -- when do we make this heartfelt love official and get married?"

"How about ... " Gordon paused in a quandary.

They embraced tighter.

"When ... ?" Sarah urged as her blue eyes searched his eyes intently.

"You know, our love is really a *special* kind of love, don't you?" Gordon said with a hint of mischievousness as beads of sweat broke out on his forehead

"Right, Gordon Smith. Exactly what kind of special love do we have?" Sarah's voice grew suspicious.

"The kind of love we should enjoy as long as it can last. We don't have to rush our love either, because of the *special* kind of love we have."

"What kind of love is that?" Sarah said a bit more firmly.

Gordon flashed a bright smile.

"Why, Sarah Nightingale ... we have a *timeless* love!"

"And ... " Sarah released her embrace and stood back one step. Her expression grew very serious.

Gordon knew he would have to choose his next works very carefully.

"Why, we have all the time in ... well, we live outside of time so ... I mean, our love is timeless so there's no need ... "

Sarah's response was swift and powerful.

"Owww!"

THE END
(Or are we in a time loop?)